P9-CAL-834

"We were both drinking," Luke said about his ex. "A lot."

Claire gave him an anxious look.

"One night she went out, with a blood-alcohol reading that was something like three times the legal limit, and plowed into a tree."

"Oh, Luke. Was she hurt? Was anyone else?"

Aside from that night at the ER, he'd never talked about the baby. Not with anyone.

"She wasn't wearing a seatbelt, so she was pretty badly banged up. And...she was pregnant, and she lost the baby."

"Oh, my God. Luke, I'm so sorry."

"I accused her of being careless and irresponsible, trying to trap me into marrying her, forcing me to have a baby I didn't want."

Claire snatched her hand away, averting her eyes.

He hated that she pulled away, mostly because he had no clue what it meant. Had he said too much? Sounded too harsh?

"She knew I didn't want a family. There's no way I'll bring another Devlin child into the world and have it grow up the way I did."

"But you're not your father, Luke!"

Dear Reader,

There's something about a reformed bad boy that grabs our interest, don't you agree? Give him a badge and a gun, and he's really got our attention! Luke Devlin, the hero of this book, is one of those men, and I have to confess to being a tiny bit jealous of the heroine, Claire DeAngelo. These two have both suffered some major disappointments since they were study buddies back in college, so when they run into each other years later, they both have trust issues to overcome.

Readers who've been following my Ready Set Sold series—the stories of three entrepreneurial young women who run a real-estate business in Seattle—have told me they're looking forward to Claire's story, and I hope all of you will have as much fun reading it as I had writing it. To be honest, it never really felt as though I was writing this story; it was more like Luke and Claire were telling it to me, and all I had to do was get it on paper. That doesn't always happen with a book, but I love it when it does!

Samantha from *The Christmas Secret* and Kristi, who you met in the *The Daddy Project,* are both back, offering their friend Claire a shoulder to lean on in *Daddy, Unexpectedly.* Since we have a bad boy cop, there has to be a villain; and as always for the animal lovers among us, there's a dog, and this time I've added a cat for good measure. And because this is the third and final book in the series, it was especially fun for me to bring all these characters together one last time and share their happy-ever-afters with you.

I always enjoy hearing from readers, so I invite you to visit my website at www.LeeMcKenzie.com and drop me a line.

Happy reading!

Lee McKenzie

Daddy, Unexpectedly

LEE MCKENZIE

HARLEQUIN® AMERICAN ROMANCE®

If you purchased this book without a cover you should be aware that this book is stolen property. It was reported as "unsold and destroyed" to the publisher, and neither the author nor the publisher has received any payment for this "stripped book."

Recycling programs
for this product may
not exist in your area.

ISBN-13: 978-0-373-75456-4

DADDY, UNEXPECTEDLY

Copyright © 2013 by Lee McKenzie McAnally

All rights reserved. Except for use in any review, the reproduction or utilization of this work in whole or in part in any form by any electronic, mechanical or other means, now known or hereafter invented, including xerography, photocopying and recording, or in any information storage or retrieval system, is forbidden without the written permission of the publisher, Harlequin Enterprises Limited, 225 Duncan Mill Road, Don Mills, Ontario M3B 3K9, Canada.

This is a work of fiction. Names, characters, places and incidents are either the product of the author's imagination or are used fictitiously, and any resemblance to actual persons, living or dead, business establishments, events or locales is entirely coincidental.

This edition published by arrangement with Harlequin Books S.A.

For questions and comments about the quality of this book, please contact us at CustomerService@Harlequin.com.

® and ™ are trademarks of Harlequin Enterprises Limited or its corporate affiliates. Trademarks indicated with ® are registered in the United States Patent and Trademark Office, the Canadian Trade Marks Office and in other countries.

HARLEQUIN®
™ www.Harlequin.com

Printed in U.S.A.

ABOUT THE AUTHOR

From the time she was ten years old and read *Anne of Green Gables* and *Little Women*, Lee McKenzie knew she wanted to be a writer, just like Anne and Jo. In the intervening years, she has written everything from advertising copy to an honors thesis in paleontology, but becoming a four-time Golden Heart finalist and a Harlequin author are among her proudest accomplishments. Lee and her artist/teacher husband live on an island along Canada's west coast, and she loves to spend time with two of her best friends—her grown-up children.

Books by Lee McKenzie
HARLEQUIN AMERICAN ROMANCE

For my two proudest accomplishments,
Joe and Michaela

Chapter One

Claire DeAngelo stabbed her fork into the last piece of lettuce on her plate. Two hours ago it was barely appetizing. Now warm and wilted, it was just plain gross. She dumped it into the trash can under the sink and put her lunch dishes in the dishwasher.

"Forget about food. You have more important things to think about." She walked purposefully back to the dining table, sat and opened the calendar on her laptop.

This had been a busy week. She had closed the sale of a home in Seattle's Victory Heights neighborhood and listed two others. She'd lined up three showings tomorrow morning for some prospective home buyers—newlyweds in search of their dream home. She would be tempted to tell them it was all downhill once the honeymoon was over, but she was a real estate agent, not a marriage counsellor.

The company she'd launched several years ago was really taking off and her two business partners were as busy as she was. Busier, given their family commitments. Claire was happy for Samantha and Kristi, she really was, but more than a little envious, too. Since she'd been a little girl, crisscrossing the country from one military base to another, she'd dreamed of a real home with a white picket fence and a big backyard, where she and the man of her dreams could watch their children chase the dog and play with their friends. Technically neither Sam nor Kristi had a white picket fence, but they had everything else Claire wanted.

She stood and walked to the floor-to-ceiling wall of glass that overlooked Puget Sound. She had a pricey penthouse with a million-dollar view, an imperialistic cat who slept most of the time, no children and a soon-to-be-ex husband. She checked her watch. It was two-thirty *and* it was Friday afternoon *and* all her work was done, so why was she feeling so out of sorts?

"Because I'm starving." The salad she'd eaten for lunch had worn off, as had the sense of virtuousness for eating something healthy and almost calorie-free. She went back into the kitchen and looked in the fridge. The makings of another salad, four eggs, a tub of fat-free yogurt and a quart of skim milk. She took out a Tupperware container filled with carrots and celery sticks, then opened a cupboard. A box of breakfast cereal with a measly hundred calories per serving and a package of rice cakes.

What were you thinking? she asked herself.

That you're supposed to be on a diet.

She set the rodent food on the polished granite countertop. Ugh.

"La Cucaracha" started playing on her cell phone. Double ugh. Only one incoming caller was assigned to that ring tone. Her can't-be-ex-soon-enough husband. She'd been hearing it a lot lately, and he was really starting to bug her. She was tempted to let the call go to voice mail, but then he'd leave a long-winded message. And then he'd call back in twenty minutes to find out if she'd listened to it.

"I told you to stop calling me," she said, forgoing the usual pleasantries when she answered.

"This is important."

It always was. "What do you want?"

"My lawyer has drawn up the divorce papers and we're sending them to your lawyer this afternoon for you to sign."

Typical Donald. He assumed she would agree to the terms, just as she had agreed to everything he'd wanted while they were married. They'd bought the luxury condo he'd chosen, postponed having a family because he wasn't ready. Getting divorced would damn well be on her terms.

"I'll discuss them with my lawyer and see what she thinks." She was suddenly overcome by the feeling that lunch had been two days ago instead of two hours, and a carrot stick wasn't going to do it for her. She was craving something rich and sweet and chocolaty. A candy bar, maybe. Or a double-chocolate donut. Or a quart of Ben & Jerry's Chocolate Therapy.

No, make that all three.

"It's a straightforward agreement," he said. "Everything will be divided equally, and we'll split the proceeds from the penthouse…although that can't happen if we don't get it on the market."

Claire picked up one of the rice cakes and pictured a Belgian waffle heaped with fresh strawberries and a mountain of whipped cream, all liberally sprinkled with shaved chocolate. "I still have to find a place to live," she reminded him.

"You own a real estate company, Claire. You've had months to find a new place. It's not that difficult."

It sure hadn't been for him. He had moved out of their home and straight into his new girlfriend's condominium. Deirdre. Claire had never met her, but she imagined the woman was a lot like Cruella de Vil, only meaner.

"My lawyer will call your lawyer," she said.

"One more thing."

With you, there always is. "What?" she asked. She

dipped an imaginary spoon into a chocolate-bottomed crème brûlée and pretended to swirl it across her tongue. Heaven.

"We've come up with an equitable division of assets, and I want that book my grandmother gave you."

Claire practically dropped the phone. *We* who? Donald and his lawyer? Donald and Deirdre? "Absolutely not. That was a gift to me, and that makes it mine."

"Doesn't matter," he said. "It was given to you by one of my family members and I want it back."

His mother had given her a butt-ugly red vinyl purse for her birthday last year. Did he want that, too? "It's a children's book," she reminded him. "Why would you want it?" Unless…was Deirdre pregnant? After insisting he wasn't ready to start a family with Claire, that would be the ultimate insult.

"Apparently it's a collector's item and it belonged… *belongs*…to my family."

Of course. This had nothing to do with sentimental feelings about families or children, or even literature. Claire still had all of her favorite books from childhood and over the years she'd added to the collection. When she finally had kids of her own, they would spend many happy hours reading those books together. Donald's grandmother had loved books, too, and had looked forward to a great-grandchild someday. Just before she died, she'd given the book to Claire and made her promise to share it with her children.

Donald probably didn't even remember it was a first edition Beatrix Potter. With him it was only about the money. *Always* about the money. Well, too bad. If he thought he was getting that book, he could think again.

No, he could go straight to hell. In a handbasket.

"It's been a busy week and I have to get back to work.

My lawyer will call your lawyer after we've looked at the papers."

He was still blustering when she hung up.

Her hands were shaking and her stomach felt like a deflated balloon. Screw the diet. She dumped the raw veggies and rice cakes into the trash, snagged her purse off the counter and headed for the door. She debated whether to leave her phone at home and quickly ruled it out. The only thing worse than getting another call from the cockroach was missing a call from a client.

ON THE WAY BACK TO HER building, Claire navigated around a cluster of pylons on the sidewalk. A window-washing platform was suspended a few feet above the ground and a crew of workers was loading equipment onto a truck.

"Claire? Claire DeAngelo? Is that you?"

She whirled around, clutching a paper bag filled with guilty pleasure. Who on earth…?

She looked up at the man on the platform and stopped breathing. She'd recognize that devilish grin anywhere. "Luke!"

He vaulted over the safety railing, landed lightly on his feet in front of her and swept her into an enthusiastic embrace. "I knew it had to be you. What are you doing here?"

"Just taking a break." She waved at the main doors of her condominium complex. "I'm on my way home, and back to work. I mean, I work at home sometimes."

He planted a kiss on her forehead. "How long has it been?"

"I'm not sure. Since college, I guess."

"Wow. Fancy digs," he said. "Good for you. And you look great."

So did he. Back in college he'd had the bluest eyes she'd ever seen and a smile that had melted a lot of girls' hearts.

She could see that hadn't changed. The rest of him had. He'd always been athletic but Adonis himself would envy this body. He still had his arms around her and the biceps alone were enough to make a woman feel light-headed. His black T-shirt was streaked with water and dust, and he smelled like hard work and testosterone. When he finally released her, she felt slightly chilled.

"Are you married? Kids?"

She shook her head, still somewhat confounded by this unexpected encounter. "Separated. Almost divorced, actually. No kids. What about you?"

She asked because she felt she had to, but she knew his answer would be negative. Luke Devlin still didn't look like the kind of man who'd ever be caged behind a white picket fence.

"Nope. Single and free as the breeze."

That was Luke, all right. The college friend she'd known and loved, and he could still make her laugh. They had met in first-year American History when they'd been paired up to work on a Civil War assignment. Claire had gone on to major in English literature and Luke had settled for being a major babe magnet. She had occasionally played the role of platonic place-holder, hanging out with him after one of his many breakups, letting the old girlfriend think she was the new one. She had always been surprised they fell for it because, let's face it, serious, studious and slightly overweight Claire DeAngelo was not Luke's type.

A number of years ago she'd run into one of his old college roommates and he'd told her that Luke had joined the Seattle Police Department. Finding out he'd become a cop had been a shocker but finding him here, working as a window washer, of all things, was a complete bombshell.

"Free as the breeze, huh? Sounds just like the old days," she said.

"Not quite. I had a pretty serious girlfriend for a while, but it didn't work out." His smile faded by a few watts.

What was this? Luke Devlin with a broken heart? Not possible. "Welcome to the club."

"Seriously? Any guy who'd dump you would have to be crazy."

"That's one adjective that works."

Luke grinned at her. "Misery loves company, isn't that what they say? We should grab a bite to eat when I get off duty. Off work. We can catch up on however many years it's been."

After the insanely busy week she'd had, and especially after that last phone call from her ex, why not? She hadn't been on a date since Donald left, which meant she technically hadn't been on a date since before she got married. Not that a casual, off-the-cuff invitation to "grab a bite" constituted a date, but it would be more fun than sitting down to a salad, alone.

"Dinner would great," she said. "What time?"

"I'm off at five. How does six o'clock sound?"

"Six will work. I'll meet you downstairs at my front door."

He kissed her again, on the cheek this time. As she walked away, she half expected him to swat her rear end the way he used to, but it seemed that even a guy like Luke grew up, at least a little. She looked back when she reached the entrance, but he'd already climbed onto the window-washing platform. That's when she noticed the red lettering on his black T-shirt. Lucky Devil, with three prongs on the tail end of the letter *y*. She was still laughing when she let herself into the lobby and pushed the elevator button. Back in college she would have given almost anything to go on a date with Luke Devlin, even though he'd had a campus-wide reputation for getting lucky. Now she knew better than to give herself to a bad-boy-cop-turned-window-washer, but for the first Friday night in forever, she had dinner plans.

LUKE TOSSED THE LAST couple of pylons into the back of the truck. *I'll be damned,* he thought. After all these years, he kinda sorta had a date with Claire DeAngelo, and he had just enough time to run this load over to the shop and get back here to meet her. Before he climbed into the cab, he reached up and yanked on the ropes to make sure the platform was secure on the roof rack. *Better change your shirt while you're at it.*

He was back at Claire's condominium complex at five minutes to six. He'd made it home in time to take his dog, Rex, out for a run and grab a shower and a change of clothes, and still made it here with enough time to spare to make it look as if he had all the time in the world. He wasn't sure why that was important, but he didn't want to make Claire wait. For one thing, knowing her, she wouldn't.

He leaned against a light standard, arms folded, and while he waited, he kept a watchful eye on everyone who came and went from Claire's building. After his years with the Seattle Police Department, maintaining a keen awareness of his surroundings was deeply ingrained. Claire wouldn't know he was a cop and given his lousy study habits in college, she was probably not surprised to see him washing windows. Just as well. It meant he wouldn't have to tell her he had her building under surveillance, or why.

She took his breath away the instant she stepped through the door. The reticent, sometimes even awkward study-buddy he'd hung out with in college had outgrown her awkwardness and blossomed into a beautiful, confident woman. She had the same soft blue eyes, still wore glasses instead of contacts, still dressed conservatively but with a lot more style.

She smiled when she saw him and raised one hand as if to wave.

"Claire!" The man who called her name was striding toward her.

She froze and her smile faded.

Okay, something wasn't right here. Luke straightened and quickly stepped up beside her.

"Donald, what are you doing here?" she asked.

"You hung up on me. We need to talk about selling the penthouse, Claire. And I want that book."

Ah, yes. The ex. The guy was a little taller than she was, very well dressed and about as intense as they come.

"Not. Now." Keeping her voice calm seemed to require some effort. "I have plans." She glanced up at Luke as though seeking confirmation.

Since Luke didn't like the look of this guy, he was more than happy to play along. He slung an arm across her shoulders and extended a hand to her ex-husband. "Luke Devlin. I don't believe we've met."

Claire's ex looked momentarily confused and then shot Luke a frosty glare. He grudgingly accepted the handshake, though. Luke didn't like his grip any more than he liked him. He was trying way too hard to be firm. For one fleeting second, Luke considered making the guy say uncle.

Don't be a dumb-ass, he chided himself.

"Donald Robinson," the guy said. After he pulled his hand away, he zeroed in on Claire again. "You can't keep putting this off."

This guy wasn't getting the memo.

Luke drew her closer. "Like Claire said, now's really

not a good time. We should get going, babe. We don't want to be late."

She looked up at him, lips ever so slightly parted, and gave him the kind of smile that suggested there was actually something going on between them. Since Donald wouldn't know there wasn't, Luke lowered his head and gave her a light, lingering kiss.

"You are so adorable," he said, purposely making his voice go soft and quiet. "Isn't she adorable?" he asked Donald.

Donald stammered something that sounded more like an excuse than an apology, and backed away. "I'll call you tomorrow," he said to Claire. "I've lined up an appraiser." He looked uncertainly from her to Luke. "Will you…ah… will you be at home tomorrow?"

"I'm not sure," she said. "I guess you'll find out when you call."

For a few seconds Donald looked like he wasn't going to let this drop, but then he threw up his hands and, without saying anything, swung around and walked away. "And I want that book back," he said over his shoulder. "I'm serious."

"Oh, my God," Claire said after her ex disappeared around the corner. She ducked out from under Luke's arm. "I am *so* sorry. And grateful. Thank you. Donald can be…"

An asshole? "Hey, no problem. I probably owed you anyway."

They both laughed at their collective memories from college days, and she seemed to relax a little.

"Any idea where you'd like to eat?" he asked.

She shook her head.

"There's a little Irish pub downtown, not far from the market. Best burgers and fries in town."

"Sure. Sounds wonderful."

He couldn't tell if she meant it or not but jeez, look at her. The powder-blue sweater he'd admired earlier was now topped by a cobalt-colored suede jacket. Both emphasized her dazzling blue eyes. She'd always had a classic style and great taste in clothes, and her taste in food was probably more sophisticated than burgers and beer. His was not and he saw no point in faking it.

"Is this place close enough to walk?"

"Guess it depends how much you like walking," he said. "I've got my bike and a spare helmet." He hoped she'd go for it. If she rode with him, he would have an excuse to bring her back home, and that would give him an opportunity to get inside the building. He was curious about the condo Donald was so determined to unload, but more than that, he wanted to see where she lived in relation to the penthouse they were staking out.

"A bike?" she asked.

"Yeah. Well, a motorcycle." He gestured to where it was parked next to the curb.

She looked decidedly undecided.

Come on, live a little, he was tempted to say. But that would get her back up and then she'd say no. Instead, he casually handed her a helmet as though he assumed she'd done this a hundred times.

EVERY SINGLE ONE OF CLAIRE'S instincts—including a few she didn't know she had—screamed at her to say no. But somehow the helmet was in her hands and then she had it on. She must look like a bobblehead, since she definitely felt like one.

"I've never ridden on a Harley-Davidson." She'd never even pedaled a ten-speed.

Luke grinned. "Then I'm happy to uphold that tradition. This isn't a Harley."

"Oh." She gave the black beast a closer look, took in the silver lettering on the side. Ducati. It still looked like the kind of machine a biker would ride, and Luke, with his longish dark hair, well-worn leather jacket and black boots, looked exactly like the kind of guy who would ride it. His jacket wasn't biker-black, though. More the color of espresso. Or dark chocolate. And while Harley-Davidson sounded dangerous and intimidating, Ducati sounded sexy. Like Luke.

He pulled on his helmet and climbed on the bike. "Jump on."

Her heart pounded in her chest. *You are such a wimp,* she scolded. People rode on motorcycles all the time. Luke was a responsible adult. She hoped. She slid one leg over the seat behind him and settled onto the cushy leather, grateful she hadn't changed into a skirt.

"Hang on," he said.

To him? she wondered. Duh. It was him or nothing. She put her hands on his sides, glad for the cool leather between her palms and his rib cage. Every nerve in her body jolted to life when he started the bike, and her pulse roared in her ears. No, that was the rev of the engine. They rolled away from the curb and she flung her arms around him, so tightly she could have counted his ribs through the jacket if she'd wanted to.

The ride to the pub lasted somewhere between five minutes and a lifetime. After he found a parking space and cut the engine, she snatched her hands away from his body and stumbled off the bike. She was both terrified and—oh, God, how could this be happening?—turned on. Being scared, yes, she could understand, but a body all aquiver from clinging to a man on the back of a motorcycle? Who knew such a thing was even possible?

Chapter Two

Luke held Claire's helmet and watched her smooth her tousled hair with shaky hands.

"Your first time?" he asked.

She responded with a silent question in her eyes and a little extra pink in her cheeks.

"On a motorcycle."

"Oh, yes. It was." He liked that the polished, professional grown-up Claire was still college-girl adorable when she got flustered.

"I thought it might have been." He handed the helmet back to her and guided her toward the entrance. "What did you think?"

"Um..." Her color deepened.

Hmm. That good. Here's hoping the ride home had the same effect.

He held the door and followed her inside. The bar was packed with the usual Friday mix of tourists and the downtown happy hour crowd. He spotted a table for two that was being vacated near the back, and before two other couples could swoop in to grab it, he was holding a chair for Claire.

She sat and slid the helmet underneath. "That was lucky."

Nope. That was experience.

The server stopped and pocketed the change left by the previous customers. "Menus?"

"Sure."

She picked up the empty glasses and put them on her tray, then gave the table a halfhearted swipe with a damp cloth. Claire's reaction had him second-guessing his decision to bring her here, but taking her to a fancier place might have sent the wrong message.

"Do you know what you want to drink?" the server asked.

The way Claire studied the drink list, she could have been cramming for an exam.

"Give us a minute?" he asked.

"Sure thing."

After the woman moved on to another table, he watched Claire suck the ripe fullness of her lower lip between her teeth, release it and slowly run the tip of her tongue across the luscious curve of her upper lip. During their many study sessions back in college, he'd watched her do that a hundred times. And he'd known then, as he did now, that she had no idea how seductive it was. She wasn't trying to tantalize, and that made it even more of a turn-on.

During those study sessions of old he had wanted to kiss that freshly moistened mouth and tease that tongue into coming out to play. But even in those days, when he had been a stereotypical college student with an overactive libido and his party mode in overdrive, he'd had enough sense not to ruin a good thing. The good thing being a study-buddy and a friend. He had never had a female friend who was just a friend, and he'd never had a study partner, period.

Their first kiss had been less than half an hour ago. He had simply wanted to send a message to the jerk of an ex-husband, but now, watching her tongue play with her lips, he wondered if she would let him bookend this date with another kiss when he took her home.

Was this a date? It would be if she let him kiss her again. Was that a good idea? Sure as hell seemed like one from where he was sitting. A kiss was just a kiss, after all. It didn't have to end with them setting the sheets on fire. Besides, he would never use Claire DeAngelo to scratch an itch, and she'd never let him anyway.

The server returned. "Have you decided on drinks?"

"Coffee for me," he said.

"Cream and sugar?"

"Black, thanks."

Over the top of the drink list, surprise registered in Claire's eyes. He couldn't fault her for that.

She set the tattered menu on the table. "I'll have a Diet Coke."

That was no surprise at all.

"Coffee and a Coke. Be right back to take your food order."

"So, Luke Devlin in a bar drinking coffee," Claire said. "That's…different."

"I'm driving."

"Of course. Good point."

"But you could have had something with a little more kick than a diet soft drink."

Something akin to alarm flickered in her eyes and vanished, leaving him wondering if maybe he imagined it. "I'm not much of a drinker."

"Me, neither."

That made her laugh.

Should he tell her the truth? *Step one,* he reminded himself. "I'm serious. I've been sober almost two years."

The amusement drained from her face. "Oh. Luke, I'm sorry I laughed. I shouldn't have."

He leaned closer and touched her hand. "No apology necessary. Sometimes even badasses grow up."

"Not always."

He guessed she was talking about her ex.

"Some of us do," he said. Too bad it sometimes took a disaster to make it happen.

She slowly withdrew her hand. "So, here we are. Ten years out of college and a couple of teetotalers."

"Wow. It's been ten years?"

"It has."

The server set Claire's soft drink and his coffee on the table. "You folks ready to order?" she asked.

Claire gave the menu another quick scan. "What's good here?"

"They have the best burgers in Seattle. The Emerald Isle is my favorite."

She read the description and grimaced. "Two beef patties *and* bacon *and* cheese? I see your appetite hasn't changed."

"I worked hard today. I need the calories."

"And I sat at my desk most of the day, so I definitely don't. I'll have the O'Chicken burger," she said, smiling at the name as she handed her menu to the server.

"Fries or salad with those?"

"Fries for me," Luke said.

"I should have a salad." Obviously that's not what she wanted.

"Have a salad," he said. "We can share my fries."

The server confirmed their order and drifted away.

"I was surprised to see you this afternoon," she said. "I bumped into one of your old dorm-mates a couple of years ago and he told me you'd joined the Seattle P.D."

So she did know. "Yeah, I got in a couple of years after I graduated college."

"And you're moonlighting as a window washer?"

He didn't want to let her believe that, mostly because it wasn't true. But because of where she lived, and the reason he was working there, he needed to be careful what he did tell her.

"I'm with vice. Sometimes an investigation is easier when the bad guys don't know who we are."

"So you're…what? Working undercover?"

He tipped his head in agreement.

"I thought things like that only happened in the movies."

"If this is a movie, that would make me James Bond."

That made her laugh. "Isn't he a spy?"

"Yeah, but it's a movie, remember? That means I get to be anybody I want. What about you?" he asked, wanting to steer the conversation in a different direction.

"Well, since you get to be Pierce Brosnan—or would that be Daniel Craig?—then I guess I'd be Julia Roberts." She was blushing again. "But more *Mona Lisa Smile* than *Pretty Woman*," she added quickly.

His turn to laugh. "Good to know, but I was talking about the real-life you. You said you work at home."

"I do, some of the time, but nothing movie-star glamorous I'm afraid. I'm a Realtor, and a partner in a business called Ready Set Sold."

He never would have imagined her as a salesperson. Then again she'd be good at anything she decided to do. "Good name for a real estate company."

"We thought so. We're more than just real estate, though. We help people renovate and stage their homes before we put them on the market."

"Good idea. How many business partners do you have?" he asked, hoping she wouldn't say her ex was one of them.

"Two. Samantha Elliott is our carpenter and general handywoman, and Kristi Callahan is an interior decorator.

They both do really amazing work, but they're more than business partners. They're my two best friends."

Huh. Three women, best friends, running a business together. He liked the sound of that. "What about Donald? Is he in real estate?" Not that it was any of his business, and he probably shouldn't even bring him up, but something about the guy didn't sit right with him.

Claire plucked a napkin from the dispenser and wiped the table in front of her. "No. He's an investment broker. He did really well at it, which is how we could afford the condo. Things between us started to fall apart right around the time the economy took a downturn, and then I found out he was…"

Luke had a pretty good idea what she was going to say, and he let her get to it without prompting.

"And then I found out he was having an affair."

Bastard. Women like Claire, and his mother, deserved better. His own track record was less than stellar but except for Sherri, he had never been in a relationship long enough to be unfaithful. Even with her, although he'd been tempted a time or two, he'd kept his pants zipped. He might be a chip off the old block in a lot of ways, but his father's infidelity had been the thing he hated most about the man. No way, not even when he'd been drinking heavily, as he had been in those days, would he let himself sink that low.

"Is that when Donald moved out?"

"He didn't have a choice. After I found out, I packed up his stuff and called a moving company."

He felt himself grin. "Hot damn, you're feisty."

He had always liked that Claire was a smart, determined woman. To know she wouldn't put up with any crap from anyone made him admire her even more. Why hadn't his mother kicked his father's ass out of the house a long time ago? Why didn't she do it now?

Claire swirled the straw in her drink. "A lot of men might think that what I did was a bit over-the-top."

"Only the ones who are cheating."

"You mentioned something about a breakup. Were you the heartbreaker or the heartbroken?"

He should have seen this question coming since he'd been the one to bring up exes. "A little of both, I guess. I didn't cheat on her, though."

"Did she? Cheat on you, I mean."

"No. At least not that I know of. We were seriously into partying and then…ah…something happened that made me realize I had a problem. I knew I needed to quit drinking, and it turned out I wasn't much fun to be with when I was sober."

"She actually said that?"

"Not in so many words. And I learned some stuff, too."

"Such as…?"

"Being sober and living with a drunk isn't much fun, either."

"Oh, Luke. I'm sorry. Do you know how she's doing now?"

"No. We sort of lost touch." Which wasn't entirely true. He did know how she was doing. Not good. He didn't want to talk about Sherri or the real reason they'd split up. He never talked about stuff like this with anyone, ever. Why was he opening up with Claire?

A food runner arrived with their order. "The O'Chicken?"

Claire patted the table in front of her, eyes widening as she took in the amount of food on her plate. The kid set the second plate in front of Luke and sidled away as the server appeared. She balanced a tray of drinks on one arm as she pulled a bottle of ketchup from her apron pocket and set it on the table.

"Anything else?" she asked.

He and Claire both shook their heads, and she carried on.

For a few moments there was silence as Luke applied a generous squirt of ketchup to his burger and squeezed another zigzag across his fries. He offered the bottle to Claire but she shook her head. He picked up the top half of his bun—lettuce, tomato, pickle and all—slapped it onto the burger side, and flattened it with his palm. While he watched Claire, he picked it up and took a bite.

She started by rescuing the pickle slice and moving it to the edge of her plate before going to work on the rest of her meal. By the time she'd unwrapped her cutlery, spread the paper napkin on her lap and, with surgical precision, cut her burger in half, he had devoured half of his.

"How is it?" he asked.

"Mmm." She murmured her approval as she swallowed.

"Help yourself to some fries."

She reached across the table, picked one up and dipped it in his ketchup. After biting it in half, she closed her eyes and chewed. "So good," she said when she opened them again. "I haven't had one of these in ages."

"Why not?"

"I've been on a diet." She picked up her fork and stabbed a piece of lettuce.

She looked fine to him. Better than fine. She had curves in all the right places, but if he told her that, she'd probably think he was lying, or coming on to her. He'd been around enough women to know that when they ordered diet drinks instead of regular, salad instead of fries and generally worried about their weight, the smart thing to say was nothing.

So instead he picked up his burger and bit off almost more than he could chew.

A CRISP FRENCH FRY AND tangy sweet ketchup were like a perfect marriage, Claire thought. What she didn't know about the latter was made up for by a deep and abiding love of food, the crisper, sweeter and greasier the better. And she had the size fourteen hips to show for it.

"What do you think of the building you live in?" Luke asked after he swallowed a mouthful of burger and washed it down with coffee. His healthy appetite and the rock-hard abs she'd clung to all the way here created an interesting dichotomy.

She twirled the straw as she stared at the surface of her drink for a moment. It sounded as though he was fishing for information, but that didn't make sense. *He's just making conversation,* she decided. They had to talk about something.

"It's not my dream home, but it's okay. We—Donald and I—bought it after we got engaged and we moved in right after the honeymoon."

She bit into her burger. After Donald's phone call that afternoon and his unexpected appearance tonight, she was more annoyed with him than ever. She still couldn't believe he'd shown up at the exact time she was meeting Luke. On the plus side, though, there had been that kiss.

"Does he make a habit of showing up like he did tonight?"

"No, he usually phones. His lawyer sent divorce papers to my lawyer this afternoon. He expects me to agree to whatever is in them."

"What do you want?"

"I guess I still want what I thought I was getting when we got married. To put down roots, have a home and a family."

"Sounds like a wonderful life." The bitter edge to his voice had a bite to it.

She knew he hadn't had the greatest home life growing up, but back in college he had never talked about it. He'd been too busy partying and playing the field. Apparently the partying had stopped, but it was too soon to tell if he'd moved past the seemingly endless string of girlfriends.

"It would be wonderful."

He didn't agree or disagree. "Do you still want that? With him?" he asked instead.

"God, no. But someday, with someone, definitely. But you don't think it's possible."

He shrugged. "I'm not saying it's *im*possible, just that I've never seen it happen."

"Seriously? You don't know anyone who's happily married?" She prided herself in being a realist, but even after her experience with Donald she still believed she had a chance at a long and happy marriage. Without that dream, the future looked awfully grim.

"Well, let's see. My parents have been married for almost forty years. I'm not sure either of them has ever been happy."

Forty years of unhappy would be grimmer than grim. Maybe that's why Luke tended to play the field rather than make a commitment.

"They're still married," she said. "That has to mean something."

Luke shrugged. "Convenience, maybe. My dad can string along his various girlfriends by telling them his wife won't give him a divorce. And I think my mom is so afraid of being on her own that she puts up with all his crap."

Claire thought of her two business partners, Sam and Kristi, who'd both grown up with loser dads and then found men who were loving husbands and devoted fathers. By comparison, she had been raised by parents who were still crazy about each other, even after all these years, yet she had ended up marrying the wrong man. Now she was staring a bleak future square in the eye.

"I'm sorry to hear your mom's had such a rough go of it. Have you talked to her about it?"

Luke pushed his empty plate away, picked up his coffee cup and leaned back in his chair. "Devlin men don't tend to be talkers."

"You're talking to me." She wondered if he would open up about his ex-girlfriend, tell her what happened there. Someday, maybe, but she sensed this wasn't the time to ask.

"True. You always were a good listener. What about your family?"

Was he asking because he was interested, or because he wanted to change the subject? Not that it mattered. She loved to talk about her family.

"My parents are in a retirement community in Arizona. You might remember that my dad spent his entire career in the military so we moved a lot. Now they have a motor home so they're still on the go."

"But that doesn't appeal to you?"

"Not in the least," she said, laughing. "Every time we moved, they did their best to make the new place feel like home for me and my sister. Carmen always fit in right away. It took me longer, and by the time I made friends and started to feel settled, my dad was transferred."

"How did you end up in Seattle?"

"I fell in love with the Pacific Northwest when we were stationed at Whidbey Island, and I decided then that when I grew up, this is where I wanted to live. Now here I am."

"And all grown-up." His voice, deep and quiet all of a sudden, like the thrum of a bass, reverberated through her.

"All grown-up," she agreed, almost breathless. And she

was having some very grown-up thoughts about the man sitting across the table.

Don't be an idiot. Luke Devlin was a man who lived in the moment, always had been and always would be. She was all about the long-term, the white picket fence, the happy ever after.

And how's that working for you? It wasn't. After months of being alone, she was lonely. Would it be so wrong to not be lonely for a change? Even just for one night? To wake up in the morning with a hot guy in her bed and a smug smile of satisfaction on her lips? Heat crept up her neck and she tried to cool her cheeks with her palms.

No, it wouldn't be wrong and she would be tempted, but she still couldn't do it. She couldn't be that woman. Could she?

Chapter Three

Luke waited for her to climb off the bike, then joined her on the sidewalk.

"I'll walk you up."

He'd had to park nearly a block away, it was dark and there was no way he could let her walk on her own. Another man might be tempted to, but not a cop. Never. Besides, he was hoping to be invited in. For the obvious reasons, of course, but also because he welcomed the chance to check out the place from the inside.

"Thank you." She sounded relieved.

On her own she would most likely come and go via the secure underground parking garage, especially at night. Not that anything was ever completely secure, especially given what he knew about the activities of some of the lowlifes who lived here. Tonight he would see her to the front door, maybe farther if he was lucky.

They'd covered about half the distance when prickles of unease shivered up his neck. He knew better than to be obvious, but a couple of casual over-the-shoulder glances revealed nothing. Someone was watching them, most likely just him, and he saw no advantage to tipping off whomever that might be. Had the operation been compromised? His gut told him no. This was about something else.

He sought out the pistol tucked in an inside jacket

pocket, curled his fingers reassuringly around the grip as his other arm went out instinctively to draw Claire closer. She glanced up, the obvious question in her eyes.

"Thought you might be cold." It sounded lame, even to him, but she didn't pull away.

"Would you like to come up for coffee?" she asked as she unlocked the front door of her building.

"Sure." Hell, yes. He was glad she'd asked. It saved him the trouble of trying to invite himself in.

Earlier she'd been on edge, possibly due to her ex showing up and giving her a hard time, and he'd thought the evening was headed for disaster. Eventually she had relaxed, and after they got their current relationship status out of the way, they had talked about work, recent movies they'd seen, what some of their old college friends were doing now and even pets. He'd adopted a German shepherd named Rex after the dog failed to meet the K-9 unit's requirements. Claire had a Siamese cat named Cleo. Cleo didn't like dogs, and Rex was afraid of cats. As they left the restaurant and walked to where he'd parked the bike, he'd been hoping that wasn't a metaphor for him and Claire. And then he'd realized that he hadn't used a word like *metaphor* since she'd been his study partner.

Not until they were stepping into the elevator did the hair on the back of his neck fall back into place. Who the hell was out there?

Claire pushed the button for the top floor. Huh. That would put her in one of the penthouses. If hers looked across to the other tower, to the penthouse his team had under surveillance, this evening might hold even more possibilities than he'd hoped it would.

They didn't speak as the numbers ticked by, and then the elevator glided to a stop and the door opened with hardly a whisper. He followed Claire into a spacious and elegantly appointed foyer with a door at either end. His luck held. Keys in hand, she walked foward and opened the door he was hoping was hers.

Inside, his gaze went immediately to the wide, wrap-around sweep of windows, taking in the view of Puget Sound to the west and the complex's twin tower to the north.

Claire set her handbag and keys on the glossy black surface of a long, sleek console table, shrugged out of her jacket and hung it in the closet.

"Can I take your jacket?" she asked.

He shook his head. "I'm good, thanks."

"Make yourself at home."

He took a good look around and thought, *Holy shit. So this is how the other half lives.* He didn't think he'd ever been in a home that was less homey. The space was huge and sprawling, with magazine-worthy living and dining areas, and an open kitchen that would hold half the basement suite he'd rented after he and Sherri split. Aside from the bare essentials, he had yet to furnish the place.

Claire had said the ex's investments had done well. Either the guy had been filthy rich to start with, or she was the queen of understatement. Or the reality lay someplace in between.

"Impressive," he said, crossing the polished wood floor, ostensibly to take in the view but instead zeroing in on his target in the neighboring tower. Bingo.

"That's what everyone says. The view is what I'll miss most after I…we sell the place."

"I can see why," he said, keeping the conversation moving while he scanned the neighboring penthouse his team had under surveillance.

Blinds obscured the bedroom windows where clients were "entertained," but the main area was wide open. With

proper surveillance equipment, he'd be able to see everyone who came and went from the place, including those
who "worked" there. Tomorrow, first thing, he would talk
to his sergeant. They didn't like to involve civilians if it
could be avoided, but this was too fine an opportunity to
pass up.

"What kind of coffee would you like?"

He backed away from the window, turned and found
himself caught in the green slitty-eyed gaze of a regal-
looking Siamese cat. This would be Chloe. She sat on
one end of the long, sleek black leather sofa, all four paws
tucked out of sight beneath her, tail wrapped snugly around
half her body. Suspecting the haughty feline would produce
one of those hidden paws and shred his hand if he tried to
pet her, he gave her a wide berth as he circled around the
island to join Claire in the kitchen.

"What are my choices?"

"You can have anything you like."

"Can I?"

Even the tip of her nose turned pink. "Cappuccino?
Latte?"

He studied the elaborate-looking stainless-steel espresso
machine on the counter. "Looks complicated. Does it make
just plain coffee?"

"Of course." She opened cupboards, reached for cups,
took the lid off a canister and scooped out some coffee
grounds.

He leaned against the island, while she turned her attention to the machine, and watched her work, admiring
the way her blue sweater curved to the contours of her
waist and hips. To his surprise, he liked that her invitation to come up for coffee really meant coffee. That hardly
ever happened. There was a time he would have nailed a
woman the second they stumbled into the apartment, and

a time before that when he'd have jumped her in the elevator. Now he was making do with coffee with the one woman he'd always wanted to make out with, because Claire DeAngelo was way too good for a dry hump in a corner of an elevator.

"Here you go." She held out a tall, steaming mug of coffee, smiled up at him and trailed her fingertips across the back of his hand when he took the cup from her.

Was she flirting? Huh. Maybe coffee wasn't just coffee, after all. Before he could figure that out, she picked up her latte cup and saucer, took a sip and smiled as she swiped the foam off her upper lip with the tip of her tongue. Okay, *that* was no accident. He set his coffee on the counter, took hers and placed it next to his and locked gazes with her.

Aw, hell. He'd recognize that smolder anywhere. And yeah, he wanted this, really wanted it, but this had to be her call. Completely. She might not want to make the first move, but she needed to give him another sign if she wanted him to make it.

Her tongue played an encore across her bottom lip.

Did she have any idea how this affected him?

Her smile suggested she did.

He groaned and pulled her into his arms. "You're sure about this?"

She leaned into him, smile gone, eyes even darker.

Please let her say yes.

"I'm sure."

Close enough.

Kissing her to piss off the ex had been little more than a boost to his ego. Kissing her for real jump-started his libido in a way no other kiss had in a very long time. Come to think of it, he hadn't kissed a woman in a very long time. Not since Sherri. Not since he got sober.

Stop thinking, he told himself, *or you'll talk yourself out of this one.*

Claire slipped her hands inside the front of his jacket. He held his breath for a few seconds, hoping she didn't encounter the Glock. He started breathing again when she slid her fingers up his chest, apparently none the wiser. Although she knew he was a cop, she wouldn't like knowing he was armed.

Still doing too damn much thinking.

Claire leaned even closer, her body soft against his. Ordinarily that would have been enough to make him stop using his head, but knowing someone on the street had been watching him still had his senses on heightened alert, and now he was acutely aware of the wide expanse of windows behind them. Anyone who cared to watch would be able to see them.

"Which way to the bedroom?"

He hated to break the mood, hoped she wouldn't change her mind, but she only tipped her head back and smiled.

"This way." She took him by the hand and led him down a hallway and into a huge master suite.

"Wow." There was a king-size bed, two bureaus, a pair of armchairs separated by a large ottoman and still enough space for a small dance floor. And the drapes were closed.

"I've never done this before," she said.

This being...? he wondered, but didn't dare ask.

"I mean, I've never brought another man here."

Is that right? Now it was up to him to make sure she didn't regret it. He shrugged off his leather jacket, slung it over the back of a chair and slowly closed the short distance between him and Claire. He watched her eyes, looking for any hint of reluctance, any suggestion that she might have changed her mind.

He stopped in front of her but didn't touch her. Without missing a beat, she wrapped her arms around his neck and kissed him.

He would let her set the pace, he decided. Even if it killed him.

He rested his hands on her hips, lightly, relishing the gentle sway as she pressed her mouth to his. Her tongue slid slowly across his lips and his resolve started to wane. For a woman unaccustomed to inviting men to her bedroom, she was damn good at it.

She shoved his T-shirt up his chest, and he made it easy for her by stripping it off and resuming the kiss. Her hands were warm against his bare flesh, and getting hotter by the minute. Time to return the favor. He tugged on her sweater and she let him pull it over her head, exposing a lacy white bra and full shapely breasts that were just…

"Beautiful," he whispered.

He backed her up to the bed, let her go long enough for her to lie down and crawled on next to her, thinking that being horizontal with Claire might be the closest he would ever get to heaven.

"The light," she said, adding a little gasp as his hand explored the lace undergarment.

"What about it?"

"We should turn it out."

"No way." He found the hooks at the back and released them with one hand, first try. Not exactly the sort of thing a guy could put on a resumé, but a damn handy skill to have. "I don't want to miss a thing."

The feel of her and the scent of her skin already had his senses on overload, but he wanted it all. He wanted to hear more of those breathy sighs, taste her and explore every square inch of her. The lights were staying on.

He took one breast into his mouth, marveling at the texture, and how the more he teased, the more it changed.

With one hand he explored her belly, hip and thigh, still clad in dark jeans. Finally unable to resist, he slipped his fingers between her legs.

Even through the fabric she was hot and damp, and he was practically delirious with desire. He hardly dared let himself believe that Lucky Devil was about to get lucky with Claire DeAngelo. A momentary flash of uncertainty ripped through him, and he reminded himself that he needed to take this slow. She deserved to be worshipped, not ravished.

Apparently she had other ideas. She tugged at his belt buckle and when that didn't give way, she ran her hand over the front of his jeans, covering him with her palm. What little willpower he had evaporated.

Next time they would take it slow. Or the time after that, for sure.

He closed his eyes and momentarily gave himself up to her intimate touch, then he undid her jeans, dipped a hand inside her panties and primed her with a couple of quick strokes.

She unzipped his fly and returned the favor.

He stroked her some more, smug in the knowledge that he was here with her, and she was hot for him. Him. He unbuckled his belt and unsnapped his jeans. She had found a way in, but he was desperate to give her full access. And she took full advantage.

This felt so right in so many ways. Sweet, shy Claire, who had always come across as being a little unsure of her womanhood, was moving to the rhythm of his touch, not afraid to show him what she wanted or give him what he needed.

His sense of personal triumph was interrupted by a sound from outside the bedroom. A key in the door? The hair went up on the back of his neck.

The door opened quietly and closed again.

What the hell?

In the space of a heartbeat his instincts shifted from the beautiful woman sprawled beside him to the disturbing awareness they were no longer alone. He put a finger to his lips, indicating she needed to be quiet, ignoring the fleeting second thought brought on by the scent of her.

His gut told him the intruder was the same person who'd been watching him earlier. In one swift silent move he stood, zipped his jeans and retrieved his gun from inside his jacket.

Claire's eyes went wide. *Shh,* he silently cautioned her again.

He moved to the bedroom door, confident that his ability to silently cross the carpet like a cat gave him the advantage. Bad enough someone had picked the lock and broken into the place, but to interrupt him when he was about to have sex for the first time in a really long time? Whoever this was deserved to get shot.

He was halfway down the short hallway when a shadow slanted across the floor ahead of him. He flattened himself against the wall and waited. By the time the shadow-maker appeared, he was ready for him. He slammed the man face-first against the opposite wall and jerked one of his arms behind his back. Air gushed out of the guy's chest with a pleasing *oomph* and the stale scent of whiskey. Luke jabbed the business end of his weapon between a couple of ribs.

"Seattle P.D. Don't move, unless maybe you've got a death wish."

"Police? What the…?"

Luke immediately recognized the voice. Claire's ex. What was this son of a bitch doing here?

"This is break-and-enter." Maybe a pat down would

teach Mr. High-and-Mighty to think twice before stalking his ex-wife and breaking into her apartment. Still, some of his tension eased, knowing the intruder wasn't one of the subjects they had under surveillance.

"Luke. Let him go." Claire appeared in the bedroom doorway, and then light flooded the hallway. She had pulled on a dressing gown and folded her arms across the front to keep it closed.

Luke lowered his weapon and reluctantly backed off.

Donald swung away from him, flexing his arm. "How can I break and enter a place if I own it?"

"By not living in it," Luke said. Did this jerk really believe he could come and go from here, from Claire's home, anytime he pleased?

"I thought you were out." Donald spoke to Claire as though Luke wasn't in the room.

Luke took a step toward him. "I don't believe you. You were sitting in your car out front when we got home. You came up here to find out what we were doing."

Donald eyed Luke's bare chest and unbuttoned jeans, then flicked his gaze at Claire. "It's a free country. I can sit anywhere I want, anytime I want."

"A *free* country?" What was this guy? Twelve? "Stalking is against the law. Maybe you'd like to take a trip down to the station and find out how goddamned free you'll be then."

"Luke. I'll handle this."

This no-nonsense Claire was new to him, and he liked her. Liked her a lot. He stood his ground, though, arms loose by his sides, ready to move if Donald decided to stay stupid.

"And you," she said, turning on the ex. "You have no business being here, and you need to leave. Now."

"But what about…"

"There are no buts, Donald. I have nothing to say to you. I told you I'll call my lawyer. My lawyer will call your lawyer. Now get out."

Luke had to hand it to her. A lot of women would have fallen apart under the circumstances, but not Claire. Her demeanor was calm and collected, her voice firm, even a bit forceful. She wasn't backing down, and she wasn't taking no for an answer. Still, he slowly reached around his back to where he'd stashed his gun. The action wasn't lost on Donald, who held up both hands, palms out, and stepped away.

"Okay, okay. I'm going, but this isn't over," he said, backing toward the door, apparently not ballsy enough to turn his back on them. Good call.

"I want this place on the market, Claire. Soon. And I want that book back."

"Out!" Claire's voice was a little sharper.

Donald opened the door, but he didn't leave. "You really a cop?" he asked.

"Yeah, I am."

"You got a badge?"

"It's in my jacket, in the *bedroom*." *You want a pissing contest? Bring it on, buddy.* "Tell you what. You want me to produce my badge, I get to read you your rights."

"That's bullshit." Now that Donald was out of the apartment, he seemed a little less intimidated and a lot more full of himself.

Luke dealt with guys like this all the time. Arrogant, never willing to acknowledge they were in the wrong, always wanting the last word. Short of locking them up, there was only one way to handle them. He shut the door in Donald's face and flipped the dead bolt home with a sharp click. Not that a dead bolt could keep out someone with keys, but Luke was reasonably confident the guy wasn't dumb enough to come back.

"You okay?" he asked, turning to face Claire.

Her bottom lip quivered a little and she shook her head.

"Come here." He drew her into his arms and held her, happy to offer comfort but feeling like an ass because now he was mostly ticked that Donald's appearance had blown his chances with her. Her breath was warm against his shoulder, her hair soft beneath his hand as he stroked the back of her head.

After a minute or two her body relaxed and she slipped her arms around his waist, letting the robe fall open as she did. He didn't need to look down to know that before she'd put on the robe, she'd shed the bra he'd unfastened earlier.

He hooked her chin with a finger and tipped her face up, needing to get a read on what she wanted from him. He didn't like what he saw.

"I'm so sorry," she said. "He's never done anything like this before."

Luke wasn't so sure. Stalkers usually worked their way up to the kind of brazen behavior they'd seen tonight. If he had to guess, he'd say Donald had been at this for a while.

"You're sure he's never been in here? Maybe when you're not home?"

Her eyes filled with concern. "I…I don't know. I just assumed he wouldn't. None of his things are here."

You're here. While Donald figured there was nothing wrong with hooking up with a new woman, he clearly had an issue with Claire moving on. Probably best not to upset her with that just now.

"I think you should change the lock." He was kind of surprised she hadn't already done that, but she had always wanted to believe the best in people.

"I'll call a locksmith first thing in the morning. Otherwise I'll never get any sleep."

"Speaking of sleep, it's getting late." He brushed her hair back and lightly kissed her forehead. "You should get some rest. If it'll help, I'll spend the night on the sofa."

"I'd like you to stay," she said, demonstrating that need by sliding her hands over his hips and angling herself against him. "But not out here."

For the second time that evening, she laced her fingers with his and led him into the bedroom. Oh, yeah. He really was a lucky devil. If anyone interrupted them this time, he just might shoot first and ask questions later.

Chapter Four

Claire eased out of a deep sleep, Luke's warm breath on the back of her neck slowly seeping into her consciousness, his body curved snugly behind hers. Early-morning light crept past the edges of the drapes, but according to the clock radio on the nightstand, she had only slept for a couple of hours. It had been a sound sleep, though. The security of having him stay the night, mixed with an exhilarating series of rapid-fire orgasms, had seen to that.

This might never happen again, she reminded herself. And that was okay.

Luke had kept her mind off of Donald's intrusion. Her ex could be annoying, demanding even, but she had never been afraid of him. This morning she didn't know what to think. What had possessed him to let himself in? What would he have done if she hadn't been here? Better question…what would he have done if she had been here alone? Luke was convinced that Donald had been sitting out front, watching them when they came home from dinner. If so, he knew she was here with another man, and yet he used his key to come in. Why would he do that? Why would he care?

She had been stalling over selling the condo, partly because she hated being rushed into making decisions, but mostly because calling the shots gave her some control over this situation. She could admit that, at least to herself. Now the idea of living here alone, even with the lock changed, creeped her out.

She needed to make a decision and she needed to make it soon, but right now she had better things to do. She was wrapped in Luke's arms, safe and satisfied, and if she didn't wake him, she could lie here a little—maybe a lot—longer.

"You awake?" he asked.

"I am. I thought you were asleep, though."

He nipped her earlobe. "I was faking it."

"You were very convincing."

She shifted onto her back so she could see him, pulling on the sheet to keep her body covered. For a little while last night she'd been a different person, or at least the way Luke had looked at her in the dim light had made her feel different. Instead of being awkward, overweight Claire, she'd been bold, even a little sexy, and she had done things with him she'd never dreamed of doing with any other man, ever. Not that there'd been many.

But this morning, in the clear, cool light of day, she was back to normal, self-consciously aware of the extra pounds she couldn't shed, not even on a diet of rice cakes and celery sticks.

"I thought about getting up and bringing you coffee in bed." Luke nuzzled the soft spot behind her ear, the way he had last night, but the stubble on his jaw turned it into a brand-new experience. "But I was pretty sure I wouldn't be able to get that coffeemaker to work. Besides…this is nice."

This was heaven, especially now that his tongue was in on the action. Her eyelids drifted shut and she gave herself over to the magic until—

"Oh!" She had loosened her grip on the sheet and Luke whisked it aside. "No, Luke. I'm cold."

"I can fix that." He pulled the sheet back over her, diving beneath it as he did.

He made her laugh, and then he made her suck in her breath, and then she forgot about everything except the thing he was doing that was making her glad she'd decided last night that she could be *that* woman.

AN HOUR LATER, SHOWERED, dressed and feeling more pleased with himself than he had in a long, long time, Luke sat on a stool at the kitchen island, drinking strong, black coffee, just the way he liked it, and watching Claire fix herself a latte. If he could convince her to let him spend some time here and monitor the activity in the building next door—and hang out with her, of course—she would have to show him how to work this contraption. It made one fine cup of coffee.

"Are you working today?" She set her cup on the counter and settled on the stool next to his. "At either of your jobs?"

"Window washers don't do residential work on Saturdays. People tend to be at home and they resent having their privacy invaded."

"Makes sense." She put a container of skim milk back in the fridge. "It seems strange, at least to me, that you actually have to be on their crew. It must be scary, hanging on the side of a building like that."

"It's not as bad as it looks." He didn't mind it, and he only needed to spend a couple of days at it, long enough to get an up close look at the penthouse across the way. "This morning I have a meeting down at the station, though. And some paperwork to catch up on."

There hadn't been a meeting scheduled, but while Claire was in the shower Luke had called his sergeant about this new development, and he had called them in to discuss the pros and cons of adding this vantage point to their stakeout. Providing Luke could find a way to get Claire to go along with it. Could he convince her to do that without letting her in on his real reason for wanting to be here? Sure, he wanted to be with her, and after last night, he figured he had a pretty good shot at spending more time with her. He knew a thing or two about satisfying a woman, and Claire was satisfied. But nobody in their right mind shacked up after one date. But Donald…that jerk just might provide him with the in he needed.

She sipped her drink, and he leaned in to take care of the foam on her lip before her tongue got to it. He liked that he could do that, loved that she would let him.

And there was that smile again. Definitely satisfied. Not that last night had only been about finding a way in here. Last night had been amazing. For the past two years, since getting sober, he'd taken his AA sponsor's advice and avoided relationships, even one-night stands. Last night he'd been more than ready to move forward, and it turned out sober sex was mind-blowing. Huh. Who freakin' knew?

"What about you?" he asked. "Is Saturday a day off?"

"Never. I'm showing condos to some young newlyweds this morning and this afternoon I'm hosting an open house at a property I listed last week." She glanced away. "Before that, I have to call a locksmith."

He touched her arm, her shoulder and finally snagged her chin, turning her to face him. "Let me call someone for you. They usually charge an arm and a leg to come out on weekends, but I have a connection."

"You have a friend who's a locksmith?"

"Not a friend." He pulled his phone out of his back pocket, brought up a number. "A contact I made on the job."

She narrowed her eyes. "Does this guy just keep bad guys out? Or does he help the good guys get in?"

Interesting that she would ask. "Some questions are best left unanswered."

She laughed. "Fair enough. If you can get me a deal and get it done right away, that's all I need to know. That, and what you'd like for breakfast."

"I never turn down a meal. What have you got?"

"Eggs." She got up and opened the fridge. "Green onions, red peppers, mushrooms. I can make an omelet as long as you're okay with no cheese."

"Sounds good to me."

He stood and picked up his coffee, making the call to Marty at Lock 'N' Key as he crossed the living room to the windows. The glass of the opposite building reflected the morning sky, making it impossible to see anything or anyone inside. A good pair of binoculars used from a discreet vantage point would change all that. He needed to make this work.

After making arrangements to have the lock changed, he rejoined Claire in the kitchen. He picked up the knife next to the cutting board and, while she cracked eggs into a bowl and whisked them, he chopped the onions and sliced peppers and mushrooms.

"You're very handy in the kitchen," she said.

"And you thought I was just a pretty face."

She laughed at that.

He tossed a sliver of red pepper into the air and caught it in his mouth. When he offered one to her, she parted her lips so he could slide it inside. He practically groaned out loud.

"I've had lots of practice. With cooking," he added, in case she thought he was talking about something else. "Comes with the territory."

"Confirmed-bachelor territory?"

He couldn't tell if she was baiting him. "Something like that. But even when I was with Sherri, I did most of the cooking. When we ate in, which wasn't often."

Claire set a skillet on the stove and turned on the element. "Do you miss her?"

No one had ever asked him that. "No, I don't. I guess that makes me a bit of a jerk."

"Being in a relationship doesn't mean you'll miss the other person when it's over. I sure don't miss Donald, especially after last night."

"Is that right? I was that good?" It was a smart-ass thing to say, but he couldn't stop himself.

Her face went from flushed to flaming in a matter of seconds, but she was grinning, too. "That's a pretty lethal weapon you have." She plucked a slice of pepper off the cutting board and slid it into his mouth. "I'm sure Donald would agree."

Donald? What the…? *She's talking about the Glock, genius.*

"Getting back to you and Sherri…" She poured olive oil into the pan. "Sorry. I don't have any butter."

He'd caught a glimpse of the inside of her fridge and noticed she didn't have a whole lot of anything. As for him and Sherri, he might as well get that out in the open.

"She's the reason I quit drinking, so I'll always be grateful to her for that. But stuff happened, bad stuff, and there was no getting past it." With the onions and peppers sliced and ready, he started on the mushrooms.

Claire poured the egg mixture into the pan. "I'm listening."

"We were both drinking," he said. "A lot. I used to hide the car keys because once she was into a bottle, there was no stopping her. No matter how hammered she was, she'd get behind the wheel, especially if she ran out of booze."

Between using a spatula to check the underside of the omelet and adding the vegetables to the pan, Claire gave him an anxious look.

"God knows, I'm no saint," he said. "But I got good at juggling the liquor so I was sober when I was on duty. Sherri didn't work so she didn't have that to keep her grounded."

"Do you think a job would have grounded her?" Claire asked.

He leaned against the counter, watching her. "I don't know. Maybe not. Probably not. Anyway, one night she found the keys. Or maybe I forgot to hide them. I'm not sure. She went out, with a blood-alcohol reading that was something like three times the legal limit, and plowed into a tree."

Claire looked up at him then, eyes brimming with concern. "Oh, Luke. Was she hurt? Was anyone else?"

"She was. No one else, though." Which wasn't exactly true, but he didn't know if he should tell her. Aside from that night at the E.R., he'd never talked about the baby. Not with anyone. Not even Sherri.

"That's a good thing, at least. Is she okay now?"

Should he tell her? Did it make sense to tell her? After all this time, here he was. Here. With her. He hadn't known how much he wanted to be with her until she'd invited him into her bedroom last night. He wanted to spend more time with her. Starting tonight, if he could find a way to make it happen.

You know what you need to do.

Step four: Make a searching and fearless moral inventory of ourselves.

Step five: Admit to another human being the exact nature of our wrongs.

Here goes nothing.

"She wasn't wearing a seat belt, so she was pretty badly banged up. Concussion, a bunch of stitches. And…"

Claire sliced through the omelet, slid the two halves onto plates and set them on the counter. "Salt and pepper?" she asked, suddenly very matter-of-fact. Very Claire.

"Sure." He took the stool he'd been sitting on earlier.

She got out cutlery and napkins, took a pair of salt-and-pepper grinders out of a cupboard and sat next to him.

"This is good," he said after swallowing a mouthful.

"Thanks." She picked up her fork. "So you were telling me about the accident."

"When I said no one else was hurt, that wasn't entirely true. She was pregnant, and she lost the baby."

"Oh, my God. Luke, I'm so sorry." She set her fork on her plate and laid a hand on his arm.

He couldn't look at her, not until he finished, because he didn't want sympathy. He wanted to move forward, maybe with her. For that to happen, she needed to know the truth.

"I didn't know about the baby. I don't know if she did, either."

"Really? How far along was she?"

"Two months, maybe a little more."

"And she was drinking all that time?"

"Yeah, a lot. The doctor never came right out and said it, but I got the impression that the miscarriage was probably for the best."

Claire squeezed his arm but stayed quiet, waiting for him to continue.

"Then I said some stuff to Sherri, and she played the victim. She was good at that and I'd always let her get away with it, but not that time. She swore she hadn't been drinking. Just swerved to miss a cat, and then there must've been something wrong with the brakes because she couldn't stop. I called her on it, pointed out that the blood work didn't lie, but she did. About the drinking, the accident, the baby…everything."

"Is that when the two of you broke up, when you decided to stop…?"

"Not quite." She didn't need to know he'd stormed out of the hospital that night, met up with a couple of buddies, got smashed. Two days later he woke up on a friend's couch with a buzz saw carving up his gut, the taste of bile in his throat, a jackhammer pounding on his skull and absolutely no recollection of how he'd spent the past forty-eight hours. If that wasn't rock bottom, if it was possible to feel like a bigger piece of shit than he had that morning, he didn't want to find out.

"I actually went on a bender for a couple of days, sobered up in time to bring her home from the hospital. I accused her of being careless and irresponsible, trying to trap me into marrying her, forcing me to have a baby I didn't want."

Claire snatched her hand away and picked up her fork again, averting her eyes.

He hated that she pulled away, mostly because he had no clue what it meant. Had he said too much? Sounded too harsh?

She refocused on him, this time with intense scrutiny. "But if the circumstances had been different…if the baby had been okay…you'd be a father right now."

That was something he hadn't been able to wrap his head around then, and it didn't get easier with time. "She knew I didn't want a family, and I didn't mean not at that particular time, and I didn't mean just not with her. I meant not ever. There's no way I'll bring another Devlin child into the world and have it grow up the way I did. Sherri knew that."

"But you're not your father, Luke."

Nice of her to say, and he'd sure like to believe it. Truth was, he'd spent most of his adult life being like his father. Getting sober had changed that, he hoped, but it was a daily struggle. Only another alcoholic could understand that and there was no point in trying to explain it to Claire, so he let it drop.

"Sherri and I talked about kids more than once and she always gave the impression we were on the same page. After she lost the baby, I stuck around, tried to work things out, but I knew the only way to fix things was to do it sober. She agreed, but I was the only one who quit drinking. So I joined AA, moved into a place of my own, got a dog and here I am."

"It sounds as though you did what you could, and then you did what you had to do," Claire said.

Nice that she was willing to give him the benefit of the doubt. Or so it seemed. He wouldn't know for sure until she agreed to see him again.

"Speaking of the dog…" He shoveled in the last forkful of omelet, drained his coffee cup. "Rex'll be going squirrelly. I need to take him out for a run sometime this morning or he'll unstuff a piece of furniture."

Claire slid off her stool and cleared away their plates and empty cups. "Why don't you go? I can wait for the locksmith. I still have plenty of time before I meet my clients."

No way. Rex could knock himself out with the arm of the couch that still had some upholstery on it because Luke was not leaving her alone here until Donald's key no longer worked the lock.

"I'll stay. Marty can be a little intimidating." Three

hundred pounds and a hundred hours at the tattoo parlor tended to have that effect.

Claire was already dressed for work in tailored navy pants with a matching jacket and crisp white shirt. They had a little time before Marty would get here, and Luke was toying with the idea of unbuttoning the shirt when music started to play.

Was that… "La Cucaracha"?

"It's Donald." She pulled her phone from her jacket pocket. "After last night, he's got a lot of nerve."

Nerve? The guy was either supremely arrogant or completely stupid. Maybe both, and that was always a dangerous combination.

"I'll let it go to voice mail," she said.

"Take it. Otherwise you're giving him the upper hand." He'd like to answer it himself, except that would be adding fuel to this guy's fire, which was already raging out of control. "Act like his showing up here last night never happened."

Claire lowered her eyes as she answered. "Good morning, Donald."

Luke stopped her when she tried to turn away. He couldn't hear what the ex was saying, but he'd be able to read it in her expression.

"I have appointments all day so no, I won't have a chance to talk to my lawyer. I'll call her on Monday." Claire shook her head. "I'm not agreeing to that. The book was a gift and I'm keeping it. Like I said yesterday…"

He could sense the struggle it took to keep her voice steady and not react. He reached for her free hand, stroked his thumb across her palm, wanting her to know she was doing great.

"Yes, I'll call her on Monday morning to set up an appointment, and she'll let your lawyer know what we've decided. Honestly, Donald, it's just a couple of days and I would appreciate it if you would stop calling."

Then she looked at him and he felt her go tense.

"That is none of your business," she said.

He knew what that meant. The son of a bitch was asking if Luke was still here. He hated this was happening to her, hated to think this jerk would now try to use him as a reason to keep stalking her, even though Luke could tell the harassment had been going on for far too long. Maybe even while they were married. Why did she put up with this?

He was tempted to go down to the lobby and see if he could spot the guy somewhere in front of the building, but this wasn't the time to leave Claire alone. He had ways of finding out what he needed to know about Donald Robinson, and he wouldn't waste any time doing it.

"I have to go. I have appointments and I have to start getting ready."

She ended the call, heaved a huge sigh and set her phone on the counter. "I'm so sorry you're being dragged into this. I don't know why he's doing this."

Luke knew exactly where the guy was coming from. He'd witnessed enough domestic disputes to know there was likely no getting through to Donald, especially since, after being caught at gunpoint last night, he was already hounding her this morning. This guy was trouble, and Luke didn't like what his instincts were telling him.

"Marty should be here anytime, so at least you know Donald can't get back in. What about your open house this afternoon? Will you be there alone?"

Her nod was barely discernible.

"Can you arrange to have someone there with you?" If not, he'd stake out the place himself.

"Do you really think that's necessary?"

"Depends on how comfortable you are with him finding out where you are and showing up."

"I'm not. I'll call my business partners and see if one of them will join me."

"Good plan." He picked up her phone and swiped the screen to bring it to life.

"What are you doing?" she asked.

"Adding my number to your contacts. If you need me for anything, if Donald gives you any grief, I want you to call me."

"I'm sure he won't—"

"Please promise me you'll call."

"All right. If he calls me, I'll call you." She sounded convincing. And then she laughed. "I'll have to find a ring tone for you, so if you call me I'll know who it is."

"Don't need one." He tucked the phone into her jacket pocket, leaned in and caught one soft earlobe between his teeth. "It won't ring when I call. It'll vibrate."

CLAIRE STOOD IN FRONT of the bathroom mirror, brushing her teeth. Luke had just left, she had a new front door key on her ring and this was the first chance she'd had to reflect on the events of the past eighteen hours or so since she'd run into him yesterday afternoon.

She looked perfectly ordinary. Same wavy brown hair, same dark-rimmed glasses, her favorite suit. No one looking at her would ever guess she'd ridden on a motorcycle, brought a man home to spend the night and had a tattooed guy named Marty change her locks.

She rinsed her mouth, then rinsed her toothbrush and returned it to its holder.

"And don't forget seeing your ex held at gunpoint."

Ironic that she and Luke had joked about the movie versions of their lives over dinner last night, and now hers felt every bit like one. But forget *Mona Lisa Smile*. This felt more *Ocean's Eleven*. Or *The Pelican Brief*.

She rolled her eyes at her reflection. "Would you listen to yourself? You're being ridiculous." This was all simply a bizarre series of coincidences that had led to a bizarre series of incidents. In a few minutes she'd be on her way to the office to meet clients, just as she did every Saturday. Her life was perfectly normal, just the way she liked it.

And it was about to get even more normal, because sometime between Donald's intrusion last night and having a tattooed biker change the lock this morning, she had made a decision. It was time to sell the condo, finalize the divorce and move on. If she left for work now, she would get to the office with time to spare. While she waited for her clients to arrive, she could look at real estate listings with her own wish list in mind.

A character home with three bedrooms, hardwood floors, a white picket fence and the world's biggest, deepest, claw-foot tub. The fence was optional because Sam had long ago offered to build one if she found the perfect home minus the white pickets.

Until then, she would keep the Beatrix Potter book in her office. She had already pulled it off the shelf and tucked it in her bag. Donald shouldn't be able to get back in here now that the lock was changed, but she had to give a new key to the building manager and she wouldn't put it past Donald to talk the guy into letting him in. She still didn't know exactly why he wanted in, if he'd been coming here all along or if this was something new, but now that he had a bee in his bonnet about the book, she would keep it locked in her office. The idea of him in here, going through her things, was downright creepy, but so far she hadn't noticed anything missing and she'd like to keep it that way.

She drew in a breath, sucking in her tummy as she buttoned her jacket. She breathed out and watched the pull of the fabric reflected in the mirror. She undid the jacket and let it fall open.

"Why won't you go away?" she asked the muffin top that was discreetly disguised by the extra layers of fabric. Still…

She turned sideways, studied herself in profile, ran both hands down the sides of her body. Luke had insisted on leaving a light on last night, insisting he wanted to see what he touched. She slid her hands back up and lightly over her breasts. *Beautiful.* Not an adjective that had ever come to mind when she looked at herself in the mirror, but that's what he'd whispered, and he sounded as though he meant it. No, if Luke had noticed her weight, he hadn't seemed to mind. Even now, the memory of his careful and deliberate exploration of her body had her heating up all over again.

"Still won't hurt to lose a few more pounds." Ordinarily she went down to the gym every morning and spent twenty minutes on the treadmill, not that it ever seemed to make any difference, but she hadn't wanted to abandon Luke. Besides, she figured the workout he'd given her last night, and again this morning, should have burned at least as many calories as her usual morning routine in the gym, which was one of the building's many amenities. She would miss that when she moved out.

"Who are you kidding?" She hated working out, but she did it anyway. When she no longer lived here, she would join a gym, maybe the one Sam belonged to, or at least buy a treadmill and set it up in one of the empty bedrooms. Otherwise she would turn into a blob.

She washed her hands, towelled them dry and opened a drawer in the vanity where she kept a tube of hand lotion.

She squeezed a small amount of rose-scented lotion into her palm, capped the tube and rubbed her hands together.

Luke had suggested dinner again tonight, said he'd call this afternoon. She got a little warmer, remembering his playful remark about making her phone vibrate. If he did call, that wouldn't be the only thing humming.

She was about to slide the drawer shut after dropping the tube inside when the plastic birth control dispenser caught her attention. She plucked it out, hating the way her chest went tight.

Had she missed a dose? Yes. Last night, for sure. And maybe the night before that? She closed her eyes and drew a couple of long, steadying breaths before she let herself look.

Oh. God.

She tossed the plastic disk into the drawer and slammed it shut. She hadn't taken one in nearly a week.

Chapter Five

Claire sat on the edge of the bathtub and let her face fall into her hands. This could not be happening. Luke had asked her about birth control last night, and she had assured him that she had it covered. At the time she'd been tumbling down the deliciously slippery slope of Luke-induced preorgasmic ecstasy when he'd asked the question. She remembered gasping yes because she was all but brainless and no other answer would have worked. And then he'd been inside her and sealed the deal on that orgasm.

But now, what if…?

She'd wanted a baby since she and Donald were first married, but she'd never missed a pill because he had wanted to wait. Now that she was single, she'd thought about stopping birth control altogether. Why bother if it wasn't necessary? But to let herself be so careless last night. How could she have let that happen?

Over breakfast Luke had shared his deep and lingering resentment over being lied to and tricked into parenthood, and at the same time he'd made his feelings known to Claire, too.

She knew I didn't want a family, and I didn't mean not at that particular time, and I didn't just mean not with her.

I meant not ever. There's no way I'll bring another Devlin child into the world and have it grow up the way I did.

It hadn't been his only reason for breaking things off with Sherri, but it had been one of them. Would Claire be able to convince him that she hadn't lied? That she'd just made a mistake? And if she couldn't make him believe her, could she live with his anger and mistrust, no matter how well justified they were?

"Stop! Listen to yourself. You don't even know that you are pregnant."

She had been on the Pill for a long time, so missing a few probably didn't even matter. There was really only one way to find out. She dug her phone out of her pocket and called the clinic, relieved they had a last-minute opening that fit right between her morning clients and her afternoon open house.

Years ago she'd seen the doctor, albeit under different circumstances, and that time she'd been given the morning-after pill. But she'd been a freshman then, young and inexperienced. This was different. She was a responsible adult, and she wanted a baby. Last night she'd been with the man she had fantasized about for four years while they were in college, and a few more after they lost touch. So okay, she *was* the woman who slept with a man on a first date. But the woman who tricked a man into having a baby he didn't want? No way. *Claire DeAngelo was not that woman.* If she was pregnant, she would figure out a way to deal with it on her own. If Luke didn't want to be a father, he didn't have to be one.

ON THE ELEVATOR TO THE parking garage, and for the first time since she and Donald had moved in here, Claire felt nervous, and it was because of him. She pressed the unlock button on the key fob as she crossed the parking lot, then slid behind the wheel and locked the door as soon as she was inside.

With her resolve stronger than ever, she called Sam and after she had her on the line, connected them to Kristi.

"Good morning. What's up?" Sam asked.

"I was wondering the same thing," Kristi said.

"I've made a decision," Claire told them. "I'm selling the condo."

"Finally!"

"It's about time!"

"Wow," she said. "I didn't realize you both felt so strongly about this."

"Sweetie," Kristi said, "it's a big decision and it's none of my business so I would never offer advice on something like this, but that place is so not you."

"Not to mention that it's time to wrap things up with Donald. Clean break, fresh start and all that." Trust Sam to be so direct.

"You're right," Claire said. "I'm kind of kicking myself for dragging my heels over this." Although if she hadn't been taking her time, chances were she wouldn't have run into Luke. One night with him had made putting up with Donald's phone calls worthwhile.

"Did something happen to bring this on all of a sudden?" Kristi asked.

"I was wondering the same thing," Sam said.

"You could say that." How much should she tell them? Would it be better to wait until they met in person?

"I just poured myself a cup of tea, Nate's taken the twins to their gymnastics class and Jenna's still sleeping," Kristi said. "I have all the time in the world."

"Me, too," Sam chimed in. "Our housekeeper just made a fresh pot of coffee, and AJ and Will have taken the dog to the park. I'm all ears."

Claire took a long, deep breath and plunged in. "I ran in to an old friend yesterday. He suggested we go out for dinner and it was…nice."

Sam laughed. "Okay, so you hook up with a guy, start making major life decisions within twelve hours and it was *nice?* That would make you queen of the understatement."

"Who is this mystery man? How long have you known him?" Kristi asked.

"We were friends in college. We never dated or anything, mostly we just studied together. Anyway, he's a detective with the Seattle P.D., he's working on some undercover assignment, and I bumped into him yesterday afternoon and—"

"Did you bring him back to your place after dinner?"

"Kristi! I'm not going to answer that."

"Sweetie, you just did."

"And now for the obvious question…" Sam said. "Did he get under *your* cover?"

Kristi laughed.

"Is it that obvious?" Claire asked. It was as if these two had suddenly become clairvoyant.

"You phone us out of the blue on Saturday morning and announce that you're selling your condo."

"And then you tell us your decision is based on dinner with an old friend."

Put that way, she supposed it was obvious.

"Okay, fine. Yes to both questions."

Her business partners squealed and giggled like a pair of teenage girls at a sleepover, and repeated what they'd said when she told them she planned to put the condo on the market.

"Finally!"

"It's about time!"

"Have you told Donald?"

Jeez, maybe these two really were psychic. The truth was, she couldn't wait to tell them about Donald's unexpected appearance last night, and Luke's *very* unexpected response to it, but that would have to wait. When she did tell them, she wanted to actually see the looks on their faces.

"I'm doing my best not to talk to Donald about anything. I see my lawyer on Monday, and I'll let her tell his lawyer."

"Good plan," Kristi said. "Will you handle the listing yourself?"

"I can't. It's a conflict of interest."

"Makes sense. Do you have someone in mind?" Sam asked.

"I do. Remember Brenda Billings? She's been selling higher-end properties in the city for years and she seems to have no problem finding buyers."

"Anything we can do to help?" Sam asked.

Claire was hoping they'd ask. "I'd love it if you'd both come over and do a walk-through with me before I list it. I don't think it needs a lot, but it's always great to have fresh eyes."

"Are you kidding?" Kristi asked. "After everything you've done to help me find my dream home—"

"Not to mention your dream guy," Sam added.

"That, too. Of course we'll help you."

"And when you start to look for a new place, I'll do an inspection for you. Check out the roof, plumbing, electrical."

The residual weight of the second thoughts she was having lifted and drifted away, replaced by the exciting possibility of finding a home that was right for her. An old character home and plenty of room for the family she hoped to have someday. *But not too soon,* she thought, experiencing another anxious twinge.

"And I'll help with color schemes, draperies and any other decorating you might want to do. It'll be fun," Kristi said.

"Have I told you guys lately how much I love you?"

"Are you kidding? You're the glue that holds this company together. You name it, we'll do it for you."

Sam's generous statement was flattering, but not even remotely true. The three of them made a solid team, and not a day went by that Claire didn't thank her lucky stars for putting the three of them at the same meeting of a group of Seattle businesswomen a number of years ago. They had met and clicked, and within a matter of weeks, Ready Set Sold had been born.

"When can we get started?" Kristi asked.

"I have some time tomorrow afternoon," Sam said. "Sundays are always quiet at my house."

"Me, too," Kristi said. "How 'bout we drop by and go through your condo, and if you've found any listings for places you like, you can show us those, too."

"That'll be great. What time?" Claire asked. If Luke spent the night again, she would need to have him gone before the girls arrived. It wasn't that she didn't want them to meet him. She wasn't ready to share him yet.

Sam was the first to answer. "How about right after lunch? We'll have Will down for a nap by then, and my mom always rests in the afternoon, too."

"That's good for me, too," Kristi said. "One o'clock?"

"Perfect. I'll see you both then." That would give her all morning with Luke. If there was going to be a morning with Luke. And if there was, she would have to add grocery shopping to her growing list of things to do today. "Right now I've got to run. I need to stop by the office, then I'm showing properties for the rest of the morning. Wish me luck?"

She desperately wanted to ask for luck during her visit to the clinic, but that would mean admitting that she'd been stupid and irresponsible. Since her business partners thought she was the glue that held them together, she couldn't bring herself to tell them that last night she'd let herself come completely unglued. Besides, there was a very good chance she had nothing to worry about. She started the car and left the parking garage.

Nothing to worry about. Hold that thought, she told herself. *Hold. That. Thought.*

ON HIS WAY INTO THE precinct, Luke stopped at the front desk, happy to see Kate Bradshaw on duty. She was a rookie, smart as whip, cute as a button and had a serious hate-on for male stalkers after a close friend of hers became a victim. If anyone would help him get a bead on Claire's ex, it was Kate.

"Hey, Luke. How's it going?"

"Good, good. Listen, I'm heading into a meeting but I'm wondering if you can do me a favor?"

"For you, anything. What would you like?"

"Can you see what you can find out about a Donald Robinson? He's in his mid-thirties, works as an investment broker."

Kate jotted the details on a notepad next to her keyboard. "This guy have a connection to your investigation?"

"No. He's the ex-husband of a friend of mine. Seems he's been stalking her."

"Son of a bitch. I'll get right on it."

"Vehicle and plate number would be good, too." Earlier that morning as he'd left Claire's building, the hair on the back of his neck was sending out a warning. It could've been his imagination, given the events of the night before, but he didn't think so. It might have been someone associated with the prostitution ring, or it might have been Donald. He could have ruled out the latter if he knew what Claire's ex was driving.

"I'll do some digging and let you know what I find."

"Thanks. I'll swing by after my meeting, see what you've come up with."

Down the hall he joined the other team members who had already arrived. Sergeant Jason Wong sprawled in his chair, his long legs clad in black jeans crossed at the ankles, nose buried in a report. He'd been the perfect choice to run this investigation. He was in his early forties, a devoted family man and hands down one of the best cops Luke had ever worked with. He could also be demanding, but he never asked more of his team than he was willing to give of himself.

Derek Johnson, another detective on the case, was hunched over a laptop and using the hunt-and-peck method to send email. Officer Patsy Smithe, who liked to remind everyone it was Smith with an *e,* was on her cell phone. She gave Luke a wink and a wave without interrupting her conversation with, by the sound of things, her boyfriend.

She had transferred up to Seattle P.D. from Portland and had been over-the-moon excited to be included on the task force. She was Vietnamese-American and drop-dead gorgeous, and she'd known as well as anyone that had been the winning combo. If they needed to get someone inside, she could pull it off. So far it hadn't come to that, but Patsy had proven herself to be one hell of a team player on the outside. Bringing her in had been a good call.

Jason closed the file he was reading and dropped it on the desk. "Luke, good to see you. After we spoke this morning, I called in the people who were free so you could run your ideas by them."

All but two, it seemed.

"Where's Cam and Dex?" Detectives Cam Ferguson and Lindi Dexter rounded out the team. They'd both joined the police force around the same time he had and sometimes it seemed as though he'd known them forever.

"Dex is holed up in a utility van in front of the building this morning, and she's not particularly happy about it. Cam's out at Sea-Tac. We got a tip from the Feds that one of Phong's right-hand guys flew in late last night, so Cam's out there going through footage taken by airport security cameras."

Derek shut his laptop and joined the conversation. "He's known to be one of Phong's bodyguards. The suspicion is that he's arriving ahead of his boss to scope out the situation, determine the security needs."

"Could be the break we've been waiting for," Luke said. They could have executed a search warrant weeks ago, after the first prostitute died from a drug overdose, but that would only net them a couple of Phong's underlings and a handful of sex trade workers, most of whom had been smuggled into the country illegally. That would put an end to this setup, but it would also force Phong and his associates underground for at least six months. Been there, done that, more than once. This time they were waiting him out.

Patsy tucked her phone into her shoulder bag. "So, Luke. Jason tells us you might have a new vantage point for us."

"I do, if I can get it to work. Turns out a…um…friend of mine has a penthouse in the next tower and it faces our target. If I can get in there with some good surveillance equipment, we should be able to see everyone who comes and goes."

"Nice to have friends in high places," Derek quipped.

"Tell us about your friend," Jason said.

"Her name's Claire DeAngelo." Watching his sergeant jot her name in his notebook caused Luke a moment of regret. Claire would hate to know she was being talked about, checked out, but it had to be done. "I knew her in college. She's a real estate agent, lives there alone. Ran into her yesterday, got myself invited up and liked what I saw."

Jason set his pen down and gave Luke a long, steady look. "You sleeping with her?"

He probably should have seen that coming. If he had, maybe he wouldn't be blushing like a schoolgirl right now.

Derek laughed. "Lucky, you dog, you."

Jason picked up his pen. "That could work to our advantage. I don't like to involve civilians if it can be avoided, but if there's any chance you can get yourself moved in there…?"

It was an open-ended question that only Luke could answer. "I'll see what I can do."

"If you work it out, call me. I'll line up the equipment you'll need."

"I can't be too obvious about this," Luke said. "Otherwise she'll be asking questions." And giving him the boot, unless he could convince her that his main reason for being there was to be with her. Which was partly true, although no one in their right mind moved in together this early in a…whatever this was. It was way too soon to call it a relationship. Besides, he disliked the *R*-word almost as much as the one that started with *L*.

"We'll make sure you're the soul of discretion," Jason replied. Then he finally cracked a smile. "At least as far as surveillance goes."

Still, Luke's mind was filled with second thoughts. He genuinely wanted to spend time with Claire. Daytime, nighttime…the more time, the better. So it wasn't like he was using her, right? He was making the most of a good opportunity. Not to mention that if she let him stay, he'd be there if loser Donald made an encore appearance. So why did he suddenly feel like a piece of crap?

Because you're not being up-front with her, asshole. He hated when people did that to him. That's how he and Sherri had been with each other, it's the way his parents operated, but it didn't have to be that way with Claire. He could be open about plenty of other stuff, so that when it came time to explain about the undercover op, she would understand. He hoped.

"Everyone have today's assignment?" Jason asked.

"Sure do," Patsy said. "I'm heading downtown, looking for a couple of girls who used to work for Phong and managed to get out."

"I was wondering what that getup was all about," Derek said.

"You got something against fishnets and platform shoes?"

"Not a thing. What does your boyfriend think of them?"

"Better not to go there," she replied. "I'll see if I can get these girls to open up, tell me how things work on the inside, who delivers the drugs."

"Now that these girls are on the outside, they might not be willing to talk. They might think it's a setup," Derek said.

Patsy batted her heavily mascaraed eyelashes at him, then grinned at Jason and Luke. "Apparently the man's not aware of my powers of persuasion."

Luke returned the smile. He'd been thinking the same thing. "I'm technically off duty today. I'm running a check on someone, shouldn't take long. Unrelated to the undercover," he added quickly. "Then it looks like I'll be cooking dinner tonight."

"Lucky lady," Jason said.

"Derek, what about you?" Luke asked.

"I'll take over from Dex this afternoon. She'll pull the utility van out of there and I'll bring in the motor home, make it look like I'm there for the night. Actually I will be there for the night."

Luke's radar went off. "Was someone from the team there last night?"

"No," Jason said. "This is our first shot at watching who comes and goes from that building. Why?"

"No reason. Just keeping abreast." And getting closer to confirming it was Donald who'd been watching him and Claire last night. They needed to nip that in the bud. If Luke was going to spend as much time there as he hoped, having that jerk hanging around could complicate things. Luke hated complications. He hoped Kate had been able to dig up something on him.

"So if we're done here…" He'd stop by the front desk on his way out, then he needed to come up with a plan to convince Claire to let him stay. Dinner was a good start, then he figured a repeat of last night's performance in the bedroom just might seal the deal.

Nice work if you can get it.

Yeah, and it's that kind of thinking that will get you into serious trouble with Claire.

He had two objectives here, and if he was going to be successful, he needed to watch his step on both counts. He'd always liked her, a lot, but things were different now. There was a chance he might actually be worthy of her. Now he had to prove he was no longer the party animal she'd known in college, the guy who coasted through with mediocre grades and a perpetual hangover, and had a hard time keeping his pants zipped. Much as he wanted to be-

lieve he was no longer that man, he wanted Claire to believe it more.

Luke stopped by the front desk on his way out of the
precinct. Kate was on the phone but she held up a finger
to indicate she'd be a minute.

"Find anything?" he asked when she ended the call.

She tore a strip off a memo pad and handed it to him.
"The guy drives a Lexus LS. Nice set of wheels. I gave
you the plate number."

"Anything else?" Luke asked.

"A couple of traffic violations, otherwise nothing note-
worthy. I've been busy, though, so I'll keep digging."

"Appreciate it." As he left the precinct and climbed onto
his bike, he turned off his thoughts about the undercover
operation and the business with Donald and pondered dinner. Something simple, he decided. He'd have to hit a grocery store, since Claire's fridge was virtually empty, and
he'd also give his dog a good run because, with any luck,
Rex would be spending another night on his own.

Chapter Six

The two-hour open house felt more like ten. Claire had just listed this home in East Queen Anne, not far from where Sam lived, and she liked to host an open house as soon as possible—it was an excellent way to get a sense of what buyers liked about the home and what didn't work for them. Today her heart wasn't in it, and her scattered thoughts were everywhere but on the job at hand.

That morning she'd shown several properties to her new clients and they'd liked one in particular, but wanted to sleep on it before deciding whether or not to make an offer. Fair enough.

Then she'd gone to the clinic, and she hadn't liked what she'd heard. After a mini lecture on why birth control only worked when taken regularly, she'd left with a diaphragm and instructions on how to use it. The doctor had suggested using condoms until the pregnancy scare was over, but she couldn't imagine how that would work. Last night Luke had told her he'd been tested for STDs after breaking up with Sherri, since he really had no idea whether or not she'd been with another man, and Claire had gone for the same test after learning about Donald's infidelity. Since they were both clean and she was on the Pill, a condom hadn't been a consideration. How could she ask him to use one now without telling him she had totally messed up? She couldn't, and she wouldn't. This was her problem, not his.

She was about to pack up her briefcase when her phone vibrated. The rest of her started to hum, too, much as it had when she'd ridden behind him on his motorcycle. As she answered, it dawned on her that "La Cucaracha" hadn't played all day, at least not since that morning. Maybe Donald was finally getting the message.

"Hi, Luke."

"Hey, you. Are you at home?"

"Not yet. I'm just leaving the open house, but I'll be there in about twenty minutes. Why?"

"Do you have plans for dinner?"

"Not so far."

"Good. What do you say I grab a few groceries and drop by, fix some for both of us?"

"You're offering to cook for me?" Another first for her.

He laughed. "Sure am. Nothing fancy, mind you, but I can manage the basics."

"You don't have to shop, though. I can pick up some groceries on my way home."

"Tell you what." His voice dropped an octave. "You go home, slip into something…comfortable. I'll look after the rest."

"Oh." The hum upgraded to a serious throb. "Sure."

"I can be there in an hour," he said. "Does that work for you?"

Yes! "Sure. Yes, of course." *Could you maybe think of something intelligent to say?* "You're sure there's nothing I can do?"

Normally she would offer to pick up a bottle of wine. If there was one semi-useful thing she'd learned from living with Donald, it was how to choose the right wine, even though she seldom drank any herself. Under the circumstances, anything with alcohol was completely inappropriate, and besides, there were still quite a few bottles in the wine rack.

"You've been working all day," he said. "Go home, put your feet up, and I'll see you in a while. Do you have a barbecue?"

"Yes, there's one on the terrace. I've never used it, though."

"And we're going to maintain that tradition."

All she could think was…wow. Luke Devlin had already proven that he knew what a woman wanted in the bedroom. But to know his way around the kitchen, too… That was just…wow. It could be that he was simply looking for an excuse to get back into her bed, which was fine by her. Being wined and dined—figuratively, at least— was a brand-new experience, and she liked it. When she and Donald had entertained, mostly his business associates, he'd loved to stand out at the barbecue and make a show of doing the cooking…after she had done the shopping and food preparation.

"I'll see you soon," she said, feeling a little breathless. If she hurried, she would have time for a quick shower before she got comfortable.

LUKE DECIDED TO LEAVE the Ducati at home and loaded the groceries into his old truck instead. He was glad Claire had agreed to dinner because he'd already shopped for the things he needed to make it. After he talked to her on the phone, he'd taken Rex for a run and showered, and now he was ready for a night out. The whole night.

When he got to her place, he drove slowly up the street, scanning the vehicles parked on both sides. Sure enough, there was the Lexus. He didn't like the weight that settled in his gut, not one bit. What the hell was with this guy?

Luke noted the driver sitting behind the wheel, then he circled the block and parked a few cars back. After five minutes, Donald didn't move, so Luke got out and, with one arm wrapped around his bag of groceries, walked up the row of cars, and rapped on the driver's side window.

Startled, Donald jumped and swung sideways. In an instant his expression went from wary to defensive.

Luke indicated he should lower the window. Donald shook his head. Luke stood his ground. Finally the window slid open a couple of inches.

"What do you want?" Donald asked.

"Here's a funny thing," Luke replied. "I was going to ask you the same question." He waited for the jerk to respond with a statement about it being a free country, but the guy seemed to think better of it.

"I need to talk to my—"

If he was going to say *wife,* he thought better of it.

"I need to talk to Claire. She hasn't answered my calls so I was going to buzz her, see if she'll let me in."

Total load of crap. "You've been sitting here awhile."

Donald narrowed his eyes but didn't respond.

"I'm just on my way up," Luke said, keeping his tone conversational. "She takes my calls. I can give her a ring right now, see if she's got a few minutes."

Donald shook his head. No surprise there. "This is private," he said. "Between me and Claire."

"Pretty sure she said her lawyer'd be in touch with yours. Monday, wasn't it?"

"This can't wait."

Luke wasn't buying that, not for a minute, and he was done listening to this guy's lame-assed excuses.

"I don't believe you. All these calls to Claire amount

to harassment. Hanging around here is stalking. Letting yourself into her apartment is break-and-enter." He leaned in close to the window.

Donald pulled himself back from the window.

"Unless you want to get slapped with a restraining order, I suggest you get yourself out of here. Don't call. Don't even think about coming back or calling. If Claire said her lawyer will be in touch, then her lawyer will be in touch."

A string of obscenities was muted by the car window sliding shut and the sound of the Lexus's engine springing to life. Luke stepped aside as Donald swung away from the curb and sped away. He watched until the swanky car and its sleazy driver disappeared around the corner, then made his way to the building's entrance and buzzed Claire to let him in.

On the elevator ride up, he debated how best to tell her about the run-in with Donald. He hated to alarm her, but she seemed to think her ex was annoying but not dangerous. Women who knew they were being stalked had a damned tough time protecting themselves. Claire couldn't keep herself safe if she didn't know what her ex was up to, or what he might be capable of doing.

Luke was willing to bet that Donald had let himself into the building after she'd gone out today, finding that his key no longer worked in the door to the apartment. If changing the lock after last night's encounter at gunpoint wasn't a deterrent, this guy truly could be dangerous.

He stepped off the elevator and all was momentarily forgotten when Claire opened the door for him and took his breath away. No need to say hello, he decided. Instead he slid his free hand into the hair at the nape of her neck and pulled her in for a kiss.

A GIRL COULD GET USED to this, Claire decided. Luke knew his way around a kitchen, and he was making himself right at home in hers. He had insisted she leave dinner entirely up to him, so she'd sat at the island sipping a virgin Bloody Mary—he had even salted the rim of the glass—while he whipped up a steak marinade, chopped vegetables for a salad and scrubbed a couple of baking potatoes.

The whole time their conversation had flowed easily. He'd had a meeting at the police station that morning, and she had shared a few anecdotes about her time spent with new clients that morning and the open house that afternoon, while carefully avoiding the details of where she'd spent her lunch hour. Then he'd told her about his run with Rex that afternoon, and had surprised her by producing a catnip mouse.

Smart man. She would have to remember to do something similar for his dog, if she ever had an opportunity to meet him.

It usually took Chloe a long time to warm up to anyone, especially men, but they had both laughed while the cat, usually so dignified and composed, had rolled on the floor with the felt toy before tossing it around and pretending to stalk it. Finally, while he stood at the counter preparing food, Chloe had made a show of rubbing herself against Luke's legs.

Quite the little hussy, Claire thought. *I guess that makes two of us.*

The kiss Luke had given her when he arrived had hinted at dessert before dinner, but then he'd shrugged out of his jacket, slung it over the back of a kitchen stool and emptied the bag of groceries he'd brought with him. She'd then sat on that same stool, sipping her drink and occasionally fingering the smooth, supple leather, wondering if his gun was tucked inside, finding the prospect strangely stimulating.

Watching a man who was this comfortable in the kitchen was a new experience. Come to think of it, the past twenty-four hours had been filled with firsts.

Spending the night with a man after their first date.

Seeing her ex held at gunpoint. She smiled.

Realizing there was a chance she could be pregnant. That wiped away the smile.

Her doctor had offered emergency contraception earlier that day, and Claire had declined without even having to think about it. She had used it once before, years ago, and it had been absolutely the right thing to do under those circumstances. As for the guy responsible for that scare, there was no question she'd been a terrible judge of character. By comparison, Donald had seemed safe, albeit a little boring, and she'd been wrong again.

This time the possibility of being pregnant was different. Not because she believed she and Luke had a chance at a relationship—there was no way this would stick and he'd already made it more than clear that he didn't want a family—but because she had loved him once, could maybe love him again. If they had created a baby together, she would love it more than life itself. She drew in a long, shaky breath and forced her thoughts back to the present, and a very nice present it was, with every woman's dream of a man here in her kitchen, making dinner for her, and clearly intending to spend the night.

The sun was setting and the air was getting cool by the time Luke carried the marinated steaks out to the barbecue on the terrace.

"How do you like yours?" he asked.

"I don't mind a little pink."

"Good to know. I'll put yours on first."

"Let me guess. You like yours rare."

"Good guess," he said with a shrug and a wink.

Claire joined him outside and after she set the table for two, she lit a couple of candles and turned on the overhead heater. She leaned on the railing for a moment, taking in the pink-hued streaks across the darkening sky and their reflection in Puget Sound. This was the one thing she would miss about this place.

Luke came up behind, put his arms around her. "Dinner won't be long."

She leaned against him, liking the feel of his body behind hers, and folded her arms over his. "This is very sweet of you. Thanks for doing this."

"My pleasure," he said. "Nice view, too."

She angled her head so she could see him. He was looking down at her. "You're not looking at the view."

"Yes, I am."

"Oh, that's smooth." She laughed, though. She'd always liked that he was so laid-back and relaxed around women, and really liked that she was now the recipient of his easygoing attention. This was fun. He made her—serious, list-making, by-the-book Claire DeAngelo—feel sexy, a little playful, even. He also made her wish this could be something more than two friends who'd figured out that being friends had certain—dare she say it?—benefits.

She could stay like this forever, but he had other ideas. Instead of becoming more intimate, he brushed her cheek with his lips and backed away. "I'll just toss my steak on the grill and then we'll be ready to eat in a few minutes."

"A few minutes?" She laughed. "That's pretty rare."

He winked again as he flipped her steak, placed his next to it and lowered the lid of the barbecue. "Be right back with the salad and baked potatoes."

She turned and leaned on the rail so she could watch

him when he came back outside. And he was a sight to behold, with a salad bowl nestled in the crook of an arm, a pair of baked potatoes in one oven-mitted hand and an assortment of condiments in his other hand.

She stepped forward and took the sour cream and bacon bits from him, then the salad, and set them on the table. "You should have asked me to give you a hand."

"No way. This is your night, remember."

Her night. She liked the sound of that.

He tossed the potatoes into the air, caught one with the mitt and the other with his bare hand, and dropped them on the plates. "Hot."

"If you get tired of moonlighting as a window washer, you can get a job as a waiter."

"Very funny." He held out her chair for her. "Sit. I'll be right back with another round of drinks, and then those steaks should be ready."

As he waited on her, it struck her that she'd never met a man who was this confident without being arrogant, this gorgeous without thinking he was God's gift. Admittedly, she didn't have a whole lot of experience in this area. She hadn't dated much in high school, and after a devastating incident in her freshman year that she did her damnedest not to think about, she hadn't dated much in college, either. Hanging out with Luke had been fun and surprisingly safe, but after graduation they'd lost touch.

A few years later she'd met Donald, and while he hadn't exactly swept her off her feet, he had been charming and attentive. It wasn't until after they were married that his charm waned and his attention wandered. Since they'd separated, his behavior had become unpredictable and, frankly, unacceptable. She had stalled selling the condo, partly as a way to get even for his infidelity, so she sup-

posed she was partly responsible, but all that should change
once they had the place on the market.

Luke set two more drinks on the table. "Be right back
with those steaks."

A minute later he was, and the steak, with its perfect
grill lines and a hint of garlic and rosemary, had her mouth
watering.

He took the chair across the table, added a generous
serving of salad to his plate and carved into his baked po-
tato. She followed suit, and for once didn't worry about
how many calories were in the salad dressing, sour cream
and bacon bits. She was pretty sure she'd be working them
off later.

She picked up her glass.

Luke lifted his and touched the rim to hers. "I noticed
you have a well-stocked wine rack," he said. "You should
feel free to open a bottle if you'd like to have some with
your dinner."

She sipped her virgin Bloody Mary and fluttered her
lashes at Luke. "Trying to get me drunk, Devlin?"

He looked taken aback. "No, jeez—"

"I was kidding. Relax. And no, I don't want wine with
dinner." A girl could only work off so many calories in
one night. "I'm not much of a drinker. Come to think of it,
I haven't opened a single bottle since Donald, um, moved
out."

Luke stabbed his fork into a piece of steak. "I remember that from college. You were not much of partier, not
the way a lot of us were."

Claire dropped her gaze to her plate, remembering those
days all too well, especially her reason for becoming *not
much of a partier*.

Luke reached across the table and touched her hand. "I
meant that as a compliment."

She looked at him, tried to smile. "I know. It's just… it's nothing."

"I know nothing when I see it and whatever this is, it's not nothing."

She didn't even like to think about that night, and she had never told anyone about it. Not Donald, not her friends, and she sure didn't want to tell Luke. It was too embarrassing. Besides, it was a long time ago. Ancient history. Water under the bridge.

"Really, Luke. It's nothing. What about you? How was your day?" she asked. "How was Rex when you got home this morning?"

"He was good. The furniture was intact, but he gave me a lecture about staying out all night."

"I'd like to meet him sometime."

"You used to jog in college, didn't you? You should run with us sometime."

"Oh, well, I don't know. I usually work out in the gym downstairs. I probably couldn't keep up with you anyway."

"Rex is very accommodating."

"I could give it a try. Sam, one of my business partners, has been after me to train with her for the marathon."

"Really? I'm impressed."

"Don't be. She runs the whole thing. I've only ever done the half marathon, and my time is never great. I only do it to stay in shape and try to lose weight."

"How long is a half marathon?" he asked.

"About thirteen miles."

"More than I've ever done." And he looked impressed as he said it. "I only run so I can keep up with the bad guys. And wear off some of Rex's excess energy."

Nice of Luke to try to boost her confidence, but she'd seen the legs beneath those jeans. He could outrun her without even breaking a sweat, and the bad guys wouldn't stand a chance.

"If you and Rex don't mind taking it slow, I'd love to run with you sometime."

"It's a date. How's your steak?"

"Perfect." It really was. She hadn't paid a lot of attention to what he'd used in the marinade, but it was delicious. "I hardly ever cook anymore. Cooking for one isn't much fun." Besides, she was usually on a diet. "So I eat a lot of salads, deli takeout, that sort of thing. What about you?"

"I never go to a restaurant or bar alone, it'd be too tempting to order a beer. I mostly eat in, but nothing fancy."

"And you call this not fancy?" she asked. She was only partly teasing.

He shrugged. "I've never done this before."

"This being…?"

"Gone to a woman's apartment and cooked dinner for her."

"Seriously?"

"Dead serious."

Wow. She didn't know how to respond to that. In a way that made her a first for him. She liked that, because she would have guessed that Luke Devlin had run out of firsts a long time ago.

"I'm flattered. And impressed." And totally turned on by the idea.

His smile suggested he'd figured that out already. "How was your day?" he asked.

"Good. Busy, but good. My new clients are already thinking about putting an offer on one of the properties I showed them. They're going to sleep on it and call me tomorrow."

"And your open house?"

She suspected he was only interested in knowing if

she'd found someone to be there with her. "That went well, too. I took your advice and asked one of my business partners to go with me."

"Glad to hear it. Has Donald called again?"

"Not since this morning."

Luke went quiet for a moment, as though carefully considering his next words, and it made her uneasy.

"No sign of him hanging around the open house this afternoon?" he asked.

"No." What did he mean by *hanging around?* "What makes you think he would do something like that?"

"I hate to tell you this, but he was parked out front when I got here a while ago."

Claire's chest went tight. She set her fork down, knowing she wouldn't be able to swallow anything anyway. "Donald was here? Where, exactly?"

"He was parked across the street."

"He was in his car? Are you sure it was him?"

"I'm sure." His gaze connected with hers and didn't waver. "I'm going to tell you something, and I'm not going to apologize for it."

"Did you pull your gun on him again?" she asked, not able to hold back a nervous laugh.

Luke laughed for real. "No, that'd be pushing my luck. I looked up his vehicle registration so I would recognize his car if I saw it."

"You can do that?"

A slight nod indicated he could.

"And you did it because…?"

"Because I was concerned he might be stalking you. Turns out, he is."

Stalking? Donald was stalking her? "That doesn't make sense. He's the one who cheated and moved on."

"It doesn't have to make sense to anyone but him. And

when I asked why he was here, he didn't have a good reason. Or any reason."

She picked up her napkin and noticed her hands were shaking. "You talked to him?"

"I did."

Luke stood, came around to her side of the table, pulled her to her feet and into his arms. She went willingly, wanting to draw on his strength, letting his warmth seep into her suddenly chilled body.

"I'm sorry, Claire. I hate having to tell you about this, but you need to know. You can't keep yourself safe if you don't."

"What did he say?" she whispered. "When you talked to him?"

"Said he needed to talk to you but you weren't answering his calls, so he was going to ring the buzzer."

Not answering his calls? That made no sense, either. "Other than that one time this morning, he hasn't called today. The way he's been lately, that's kind of unusual but I figured..." Truth was she'd been feeling rather smug about it, assuming now that Donald knew she was seeing someone, he was backing off.

"I don't think he had any intention of buzzing. He knew you were here, though. I'm sure of that. He was waiting to see if I showed up."

"Are you sure? Maybe there's some other explanation—" She desperately wanted there to be. The thought of her ex-husband sitting out there in his car, watching the building, knowing when she was out and when she was home...

Her gaze darted to the railing and beyond. The terrace wasn't visible from the street. From here they couldn't even be seen from the complex's other tower. Silly to worry, to feel exposed out here, but still she shuddered.

Luke must have felt it, too, because he drew her even closer. He didn't say anything, though. He just held her. She would never have guessed he could be like this. Gentle, comforting, and in a nonsexual way. She didn't know why that surprised her, but it did. She wrapped her arms around his waist, nestled closer and pressed her face against his shoulder. This felt so good, so right. There was nothing she could do about Donald right now, but there was something she could do about this.

"Let's go inside."

"You've had enough to eat?"

"Mmm-hmm. Now I'm ready for the next course." She tipped her head back and he lowered his at the same time. The kiss they shared was filled with give-and-take, and for maybe the first time in her life, she wasn't afraid to show a man that, yes, she wanted him, but she also needed to feel safe, secure, sheltered from the world, at least for tonight. Tomorrow would take care of itself.

Chapter Seven

Dessert always had been Luke's favorite course. They'd finished dinner several hours ago. Now, just minutes shy of midnight, he lay next to Claire, spent and relaxed, satisfied the same was true for her, and certain there was no sweeter way to end dinner with a beautiful woman. With her back against his chest and his arm limp across her waist, he could feel her breathing slowly grow shallow and even.

Years ago his knack for charming the ladies had earned him the nickname Lucky. Truth was, he'd been careless and irresponsible, and if he had one regret, it was that he couldn't turn back the clock and undo all the moronic things he'd done while he was drinking. Getting sober had kick-started his conscience, though. At first he'd tried to justify all of it by using the booze as an excuse, but over time he'd come to realize there was no was excuse. He'd done a lot of shitty things, he needed to own them, and when he could, he had to try to make amends for them.

Being here with Claire felt right in just about every way possible, starting with the fact that she was one of the few women—hell, maybe the only woman—who had somehow looked past his flaws and been friends with him anyway. He had wanted to make love to her during their days of being study-buddies, but something had held him back. Maybe because he'd always been sober, more or less, for their study sessions and had enough sense to know he didn't deserve to have her. Claire wasn't a one-night stand, and other than Sherri, those one-night stands were what he'd done best.

With the tip of a finger he slowly, lightly drew circles around her navel and thanked his lucky stars he'd never screwed things up with her.

Something had happened in her past, though. Over dinner he'd made an off-the-cuff comment about her not being much of a partier. He hadn't anticipated her reaction, but it was one he'd seen before. Sadly, it was one that every cop saw way too often. Victims of domestic violence, sexual assault, rape—no matter who they were or what the circumstance, they had one thing in common. It was *that* reaction, and it was always *nothing*.

Oh, shit.

What if he…?

Had he ever…?

Shit.

Claire shifted against him. "Is something wrong?"

"No. Why do you ask?"

"You got tense all of a sudden. Did you hear something?"

"Everything's fine," he whispered against her hair. Except it wasn't, not by a long shot, and he needed to clear the air.

"Earlier, when I asked you if something had happened, you said it was nothing. I didn't buy it, and then I got to thinking about all the stupid stuff I used to do. All the partying and drinking. And that got me wondering, when we were in college, did I—?"

Claire rolled over, and in the dim light cast by a single bedside lamp, he tried to read the reaction in those midnight-blue eyes.

He kept an arm around her because he was sure that no matter how she answered his next question, the truth would be in her physical response.

"Was it me? Did I ever come on to you or…" God, this was hard. "Or something worse?"

For a split second her eyes went wide, then softened along with the rest of her. She touched a hand to the side of his face, kissed him lightly on the lips. "Never." Then she smiled. "I used to wish you'd ask me out.…"

That was a surprise. He'd had no idea.

"But you never did," she said. "You didn't do anything else, either. What made you ask?"

"I was a jerk back then. Young, stupid. Drank too much too often, woke up some mornings with no memory of what I'd done the night before. I'd hate to think I ever did anything to hurt you."

"Of course you didn't. We were just friends."

He drew her closer and returned the kiss she'd given him. "So what happened to you?"

"I… What makes you think anything happened?"

"I'm a cop. I see women's reactions to certain things. Yours was textbook." He still wasn't sure she would tell him, though, until he heard her sigh.

"It was a long time ago, freshman year to be exact. FYI, I didn't even know you then. I went to a party in one of the dorms. To say I wasn't used to drinking would be the understatement of the century, but there was this boy and I wanted him to think I was cool.

"I woke up the next morning with the hangover from hell. I didn't know whose room I was in, but I was alone. My underwear was on the floor and I had no idea if he used any kind of protection. When I got back to my dorm, my roommate dragged me off to the campus clinic. And after that—" She gave a nervous laugh. "As you said, I've never been much of partier."

"Did you remember what happened?"

She shook her head. "Vaguely."

Sounded like maybe she'd been roofied. "Did you press charges?"

"No. At the time I believed it was as much my fault as his. We were both drunk. Maybe if I hadn't had so much to drink—"

"It wasn't your fault." He hated that women believed that.

"I know that now. But then I was young, naive, and I think I was more upset about losing my dignity and self-respect than my virginity."

Anger rumbled through him. There'd been plenty of girls in college who were willing to jump into bed with a guy. Hell, he'd made out with plenty of inebriated girls at parties, sometimes went all the way with them, but he had never crossed that line, never forced a girl to give it up against her will.

Not that you can remember, anyway. What about all those morning-afters when he had no memory of what the hell he'd done the night before? And who was to say that wasn't a selective memory? Anger was suddenly overcome by guilt.

"I feel like I should apologize for the entire male species. We can be idiots." Maybe apologizing to her was a way to make good for his past indiscretions.

She snuggled closer, laughing softly. "Sorry, that's one apology I can't accept."

"Why not?"

"Because you're not responsible for half the human race.

Besides, I'm okay. I learned that I needed to look out for myself, that it was up to me to keep myself safe."

Her comment shifted his thoughts to Donald, and he suspected hers went there, too. Tonight he had planned to discuss moving in here, but an opportunity hadn't presented itself and now wasn't the right time. He'd wait until tomorrow, over breakfast, maybe. If he had to, he'd create an opportunity.

"I hope you don't mind me saying this," Claire said. "But this is something Donald and I never did together."

Luke and Claire had done a lot of things since they'd stumbled into the bedroom tonight. He wasn't sure which of them she meant. "I'm afraid you'll have to be more specific." He stroked the hair back from her forehead and tucked it behind her ear.

"Pillow talk."

He was already acutely aware that another man had shared this bed with her. Now the periodic pangs of jealousy that'd been elbowing him in the gut were chased away by a smug sense of superiority. No question he'd satisfied her sexually, but emotionally? As far as he knew, that was a first. The old Luke would have been scared witless by that, but this new-and-improved—or so he hoped—version of himself liked the idea. A lot. There might be some depth to his character, after all.

"Pillow talk, huh? That's what you call this?"

Somehow, without him noticing, she'd slipped a hand around him and now it was slowly exploring the contours of his backside.

"What would you call it?" she asked.

For the briefest of instances, surely no more than a millisecond, the *L*-word flashed through his brain. No freaking way was he calling it that. That would be crazy. Make that insane.

"Pillow talk works for me."

"Good." That hand of hers got a little bolder. "What about this? Does this work?"

With his arms around her, he flipped onto his back and rolled her on top of him. "I was thinking we should get some sleep."

"Really?" She smiled down at him. "You don't *feel* sleepy."

She definitely knew how to keep a guy awake. "Are you saying you've had enough pillow talk for one night?"

"That's what I'm saying."

He took her face in his hands and kissed her, long and deep. There'd be plenty of time for talking. Tomorrow.

CLAIRE WAS CLEARING away their breakfast dishes, although it was close to noon, when "La Cucaracha" blared from her phone. *Now what?* she wondered as she picked it up. Luke was out on the terrace gathering up last night's dishes but he must have heard it, too, because he appeared immediately.

"What do you want, Donald?"

"I wanted to find out what time you're meeting with your lawyer tomorrow."

That was the best excuse he could come up with? Talk about lame. "I don't have an appointment yet," she said, trying to keep her tone pleasant. Given his behavior of late, there was no sense in antagonizing him. "I'll call her office first thing in the morning and set something up."

Luke came up behind her and quietly set a stack of dishes on the counter.

"Why didn't you do that on Friday?" Donald asked.

"I was busy." Which wasn't exactly true. She'd run into Luke and everything else had completely slipped her mind.

"We need to get the condo listed, Claire. It could take months to find a buyer."

"I'm working on it."

There was a long pause before Donald spoke. "Really? I know someone—"

"I already have an agent in mind. If I'm going to do this, I want someone I can—" She almost said *trust,* but that would really get Donald riled. "I want someone I know."

This could be tricky. Having a lockbox with a key would make it easier for Donald to get in, and just the thought of it had her feeling queasy. They would have to make the showings by appointment only.

"Fine," he said. "At this point I don't even care. I want to get my money out of that place."

A car horn blared in the background, and Claire could have sworn it echoed the same piercing sound that rose up from the street and through the terrace doors. She pointed outside, silently mouthing to Luke that she thought her ex was down there.

He strode through the apartment, across the terrace to the railing and scanned the street below.

"Claire? Are you still there?"

"Yes. Yes, I'm here. Sorry, I got distracted."

Luke turned to face her, gave a single nod. His mouth, with those magic lips, usually so expressive, so ready with the quirky smile, was pressed into a grim line.

"Um, listen, I really should go. Sam and Kristi are coming over for coffee and I need to get ready for them."

"So you're alone right now?"

How to answer that? If she said she was alone, he might want to come up. If he knew Luke was here...

Who was she kidding? Donald had been out there when Luke got here yesterday. For all she knew, he'd spent the night out there, waiting to see if he'd left. Would he do that? Sit there all night? Why? Why did he care? And what about Deirdre? Luke was right. Something wasn't right and for the first time in her life, Claire was truly afraid. Make that terrified.

"Claire! I asked you if—"

"I have to go, Donald." She ended the call without answering his question and as her shaky fingers let her phone clatter to the counter, she sagged into Luke's arms.

LUKE HAD BEEN WAITING for a window of opportunity to appear, and that crazy son of a bitch had just flung it wide open.

"Why is he doing this?" Even muffled against his chest, there was no mistaking the panic in Claire's voice.

He held her close, hoped she wasn't going to cry. He'd never been good with crying women. "I don't know. He probably doesn't know, either, although I guarantee he's cooked up a story to justify what he's doing."

"What should I do? Get a restraining order?"

"It's not that easy." He smoothed her hair, hoping she found it comforting. "To do that, you would have to provide evidence that he's threatened you or that he poses a threat in some way."

"What about my phone records? That would show how often he's been calling. And then there's the other night, when he came in here."

"The phone calls won't be enough. He could say those were necessary."

Claire pulled back and looked up at him. "Necessary?"

"I'm not saying they were, but he could argue they were about the divorce, the property settlement and that you've been stalling."

"Hey, whose side are you on here?" She tried to pull away.

He kept her close. "Yours, of course, but I'm being re-alistic."

"It's not helping."

"I might have a solution."

"Really? What it is it?"

He hesitated, hoping she wouldn't be offended, or think he was trying to take advantage of the situation to make a move on her.

"I'm all ears, Luke."

"I could stay here for a bit, at least until you talk to your lawyer and real estate agent and get all that stuff sorted out. Maybe that's all it'll take to get Donald to back off."

"You want to move in?"

"When you put it like that, it sounds awfully—"

"Fast?"

"Yeah, fast." Speed-of-light fast.

She was smiling. "What would we tell people? That we're a couple? Or that you're my bodyguard?"

She was messing with him. He hoped. And exactly which people was she referring to? "Do we need to tell them anything?"

"I guess not. Unless they ask, and then maybe we should have our stories straight."

The plan wasn't five minutes old and already it was complicated. He hated complicated. He wanted to moni-tor the activity in the neighboring penthouse, he wanted to be with her and he wanted to keep her safe.

Right. That didn't sound complicated at all.

"Do we need a story? Maybe we just say we're seeing each other and let people draw their own conclusions. It's not like I'll be moving all my stuff in."

"And are we 'seeing each other'? I mean, it's been less than forty-eight hours since we bumped into each other."

And they'd bumped into each other a lot since then.

"What about your dog?"

He hadn't factored Rex into the equation. "My landlady will look after him for however long this takes, and I can still swing by and take him for a run. His nose'll be out of joint, but he'll get over it."

"You could bring him here."

"I don't know. He's a big dog. And what about Chloe?" He'd won her over with a catnip mouse. He had a feeling it would take a lot more than that to get her to warm up to an eighty-pound German shepherd with a mild inferiority complex.

"It'll be good for her. After I move into a place of my own, I'd like to get a dog. Having Rex here would help her get used to having one around."

"I guess it can't hurt to give it a try." He could always take Rex back to his place if it didn't work out.

"I work from home some of the time, so I could take him for walks."

"Rex would like that." And this could have a plus side. Being nabbed at gunpoint hadn't discouraged Donald. Maybe the idea of a canine takedown would make him think twice. But the biggest plus was that she'd agreed to let Luke stay. He was in, she had agreed to it without hesitation and she didn't seem to suspect he had any other motivation for wanting to be here. Not that being with her and keeping her safe weren't important; they were. But would those things alone have been enough to prompt him to take such a big step, and so soon? Not a chance.

Now, looking down into Claire's smiling blue eyes, seeing the trust she had in him, gave a little more edge to the already sharp guilt pangs he was feeling. How would she react if she found out he'd deceived her? She'd boot his ass out of there so fast, he wouldn't even it see it coming.

"I should finish cleaning up the kitchen." She slipped

out of his arms and opened the dishwasher. "Sam and Kristi, my business partners, are coming over. They're going to help me get the condo ready to put on the market."

The place already looked like a show home, and he found it hard to imagine how they would improve on that.

"I have stuff I need to do, too, so I'll clear out and leave you ladies to do your thing. I won't leave until they get here, though."

"I appreciate that. I'm not quite ready to be here on my own just yet."

He hadn't wanted to mention Donald again so he was glad they were on the same page. "I'll bring in the rest of the dishes from the terrace."

"Thanks." She was already rinsing plates and cutlery.

Outside, Luke loaded glasses, napkins and several other items onto the tray Claire had left on the polished tile counter next to the built-in barbecue. This outdoor kitchen was better equipped than most indoor kitchens. It even had a sink and running water. He'd never seen anything like it. And while this wasn't the sort of place he'd have pictured Claire living in, it was a reminder that they were from different worlds. He had never really considered buying a place of his own, but if he did, this sure wouldn't be it. Not on a cop's salary.

After checking to be sure Claire was occupied, he glanced over the rail at the street below. The Lexus was gone. He'd known it was Donald's car because the guy had been standing on the sidewalk next to it while he was on the phone harassing Claire. Luke had another meeting with Wong and the rest of the team early that afternoon, and he'd definitely check with Kate Bradshaw again to see if she'd dug up any more dirt on this guy. For Claire's sake, he hoped they didn't find anything, but it sure wouldn't surprise him if they did.

Claire's phone went off as he carried the tray inside and set it on the counter. Not the cockroach, thank God.

"That's Sam and Kristi," Claire said. "They're just texting to let me know they're almost here." She took the tray from him. "I know you have things to do, so you don't need to hang around. I'll be fine for a few minutes on my own until they get here."

This was an interesting development. "So, you don't want me to meet your friends? Or you don't want them to meet me?"

"Of course I want them to meet you." She set the tray on the counter, put her arms around his neck, did her best to give him a seductive little smile. "Eventually. I'm just not ready to share you yet."

She stopped talking and he watched her face turn pink. Adorable.

"You're a pretty little liar," he said. "Did you know you blush when you're not telling the truth? It's cute."

The pink turned to red. "Okay, fine. It's just that this—us—it's so new, and you don't know those two." She rolled her eyes. "Of course you don't know them. You haven't met them. What I mean is, they're both in relationships, really solid ones, and if they meet you now, here, on Sunday morning, they'll assume you spent the night here—"

"I did spend the night here." He probably shouldn't be enjoying this as much as he was.

"They don't need to know that. They'll jump to all sorts of conclusions and I'll never hear the end of it."

"So you're worried they'll take one look at me and tell you to make a run for it?"

She laughed. "You really can be a devil, Luke Devlin. You know perfectly well what women think when they see you."

He shouldn't tease her, but who could resist? He lowered his head and brushed her lips with his. "Listen, darling. If one of your friends makes a pass at me, I promise I'll let her down easy."

He loved hearing her laugh. "You're hopeless," she said. "But you can stay, as long as you promise to behave."

He took her hand in his and drew a cross over his heart. "Oh, I'll be good. I promise."

The buzzer announced her friends' arrival. Saved by the bell. Initially he had only wanted to stay until they got here so he could be sure Donald wouldn't have an opportunity to get to her while she was alone. Now he was curious to meet these women, and yes, he would be on his best behavior because suddenly it was important that he make a good impression.

Chapter Eight

Claire opened the door to her two best friends and an enormous bouquet. Kristi, holding the flowers, gave her a one-armed hug. Sam, with her trusty clipboard in hand, hugged her with both arms. Then Kristi thrust the flowers into her hands.

"Oh, my goodness. These are beautiful. I love roses. But what have I done to deserve flowers?"

"Think of them as an early housewarming present," Kristi said.

"And an overdue good-riddance-to-Donald gift." Just like Sam to shoot straight from the hip.

Kristi jabbed her with an elbow. "Be nice."

Sam grinned. "I am. You'd know that if you heard what I really wanted to say."

As always, these two were a breath of fresh air, and their visit was exactly what she needed right now. Usually the steady one, she now needed someone else to keep her grounded.

"Come in. Luke's here, just leaving, actually, but I'd like you to meet him." Then she dropped her voice to a whisper. "And be nice…both of you."

"Oooh." Sam and Kristi bumped shoulders and exchanged looks.

"Of course we'll be nice."

"We're always nice."

Luke had his jacket on and was leaning against the island when Claire led them into the kitchen. Chloe had jumped onto the counter and was brushing the side of her face on his shoulder. The little flirt.

The smile he gave Claire would have had her shedding some clothes if they were alone.

"Luke." She was having difficulty breathing, as if she'd just run up a flight or two of stairs. Or ten. "These are my friends and co-owners of Ready Set Sold. Sam is our carpenter, and Kristi is the interior decorator."

The smile he gave them was disarming but in a completely different way. The handshake he shared with Sam was brief and businesslike, a little reserved, even. Claire could see she was quietly assessing the man.

With a nod, Sam stepped back. "Good to meet you."

Claire took a quick breath, unaware she'd been holding it.

Kristi was all smiles. She shook Luke's hand for far too long to be strictly professional but not long enough to send the wrong message. "Very nice," she said. "To meet you. Very nice to meet you."

"Pleasure's all mine," he said. "I wish I could stay but I understand you ladies have work to do, and I have a meeting this afternoon myself."

Kristi all but giggled, and even Sam was getting soft around the edges.

"I'll walk you out." Claire shooed the cat off the counter and reached for his sleeve.

He caught her hand in his, briefly held both it and her gaze hostage, then slipped his arm around her. "Good plan. Sam, Kristi," he said over his shoulder. "I hope I see you again soon."

"Oh, yes."

"Absolutely."

"For sure."

"Soon."

Like a pair of silly schoolgirls. And who could blame them?

At the door, Luke turned her into his arms. "Your friends are watching," he said, low enough that only she could hear.

"I figured they would be."

"Okay, just as long as you know." And with one hand on the back of her head and the other on her butt, he drew her into an intimate embrace and a kiss that really wasn't meant to go public.

"I'll call you about dinner," he said after he lifted his head. "And…" He glanced up at their audience and smiled. "And that other thing we talked about."

He let himself out, and left Claire with lots of explaining to do.

Sam and Kristi both rushed into the foyer, grabbed her by the arms and hauled her back to the kitchen.

"Oh. My. God." Kristi sounded very much like Jenna, her fourteen-year-old daughter. "I… I'm…"

"I think what she's trying to say is, wow," Sam said.

"Holy handsome hunk of wow," Kristi added.

Claire knew she was sporting a foolish grin and she didn't care. Kristi's description summed him up just about perfectly.

Sam urged her onto a stool and stepped back to look at her. "That was some kiss."

"Those were some abs," Kristi said. "And pecs, and—"

"He was wearing a jacket," Claire reminded her. "And a shirt. You did not see abs and pecs."

"Didn't have to. That man's got it all…abs, pecs, biceps.

Don't even think about telling us otherwise. We won't believe you."

"I wouldn't dream of it." She couldn't have kept the smug out of that reply if she'd tried. He was pretty much perfect in every possible way.

Kristi slid onto the next stool. "Now let's have it, and don't you dare spare a detail."

"No way. You know the Ready Set Sold rules. Business first, chitchat later."

"Evil taskmaster." Sam set her clipboard on the counter, leaned on her elbows and groaned. "I think we can make an exception, just this once."

"I agree," Kristi said. "This is just too delicious to postpone."

Claire gave them a firm head-shake. "No way. We never made that exception for either of you. Not when we found out you and AJ were long-lost lovers," she said to Sam. "Not when Kristi told us she and Nate were fake dating, either, and we're not breaking the rule for me."

"Fine." Kristi pretended to pout. "But if I have to work, I'm going to need a cup of tea."

"Of course." Claire slid off her stool and walked around to the kitchen side of the island. "Sam, I'll make you some coffee."

"Oh, um, no thanks. Unless you have decaf."

Sam drinking decaf? That never happened. Claire eyed her suspiciously as she filled the kettle, and noticed Kristi was doing the same.

"What's up with you?" Kristi asked.

"Nothing." Sam shrugged to support her claim, but her cheeks turning pink suggested otherwise.

"Oh. My. God." Kristi clapped her hands together. "You're pregnant!"

Still feigning innocence, Sam eyed the package on the counter. "Are those bagels?"

Claire switched on the kettle. "Sam? Are you?"

Now completely red in the face, Sam grinned. "We are. AJ and I decided to keep it to ourselves until we were through the first trimester, just in case—"

Claire and Kristi rushed at her from both sides and then they were group-hugging and shedding happy tears.

"I can't believe you kept this from us!"

"When did you find out?"

"How far along are you?"

"Three months," Sam said, laughing and crying at the same time. "We just told Will this morning that he's going to have a baby brother or sister."

"How did he take it?"

"Is he excited?"

"He asked if we were getting another dog, too. He says the baby should have a puppy of its own, but we really think he just wants another dog."

"That is too funny," Kristi said. "And I am so, so happy for you."

"Me, too. AJ must be thrilled."

"Beyond thrilled," Sam said. "He's been to all my doctor's appointments with me, and he was there for the sonogram last week. Oh, that reminds me. I have it with me." She retrieved it from under the sheets of paper on her clipboard.

Kristi went misty-eyed. "Oh, I want one," she said as she gazed at the mottled grey image.

"Have you and Nate talked about it?" Sam asked.

"We have, and we've decided to wait. We've just blended our two families and it's going really well. Jenna's crazy about her new little sisters and the twins absolutely adore her, but it's still a big adjustment so we'll hold off a bit before we add a baby to the mix."

Somewhat reluctantly, Claire accepted the photograph when Kristi handed it to her. She had been trying not to think about her own predicament, but Sam's news brought it all back in a rush. Now, suddenly feeling a little lightheaded, a little queasy, even, she backed herself onto a stool and sat down. *It's just nerves,* she told herself. This was way too soon for morning sickness, or so the doctor said.

The boiling kettle snapped her back to the present. "Teatime," she said. "I'll make you a decaf, Sam. And a latte for myself." *Better make that a decaf latte,* she thought. *Just in case.*

"I still have my eye on one of those bagels," Sam said. "You won't believe the appetite I have these days."

"Help yourself. There's cream cheese in the fridge."

There was no missing the looks exchanged by her friends.

"Bagels and cream cheese?"

"In *this* kitchen?"

"Do you think we've somehow stumbled into a parallel universe?" Sam asked Kristi.

"Knock it off, you two. Luke brought them."

"Makes sense. You can't expect a man with a body like that to live on rabbit food."

"I'll have you know I've lost two pounds." She'd gone into the bathroom and weighed herself that morning while Luke was still in bed, and she was practically giddy about it.

"Good for you."

She opened a cupboard, took out mugs and plates. "To be honest, I'm not sure how it happened. I've been starving for weeks and haven't lost an ounce. This weekend I totally fell off the wagon, haven't been watching what I've been eating, and I'm down two pounds. Two point two, to be precise."

Sam and Kristi traded another knowing glance.

"Don't start, you two," she warned. "Don't even think about it."

Sam feigned surprise, Kristi sealed her lips with an imaginary key and tossed it over her shoulder, and they grinned at each other again.

But Claire couldn't help thinking about it. Even though it was just a couple of pounds, she felt different. Not thinner, but she did feel… *Okay, go ahead, let yourself think it. Sexy.*

She made a decaf Americano for Sam and a skinny decaf latte for herself—just in case—while the kettle boiled for tea. When the drinks were ready, she set them on a tray. "Let's sit at the dining room table."

The dining room was not so much a room as an area defined as such by the presence of a large, sleek table and eight high-backed parsons' chairs. It was bordered on one side by the back of the leather sofa in the living area, and on another by the floor-to-ceiling windows overlooking Puget Sound.

Kristi picked up her tea. "I do love this view."

"It's a major selling feature," Sam said. "Not really my thing, though. I love the view of Lake Union from our place, but at the same time we still have a lot of privacy. Having that other tower right there, wondering who's behind those windows and whether or not they can see us…" To make her point, she gave a little shudder. "It's kind of creepy."

Until a few days ago, Claire hadn't given it much thought. Now, knowing that Donald was hanging around, possibly even coming inside the apartment when she wasn't here, she was creeped out, too, but for different reasons. It was time to move on.

She had noticed that Luke seemed interested in the view, especially from the windows that faced the next tower. That's where she'd seen him with the window-washing crew, so it might have something to do with that. He hadn't said anything more about looking into that company and since it was part of a police investigation he probably couldn't, but she assumed he'd be back there on Monday. At least he wouldn't have far to go to work, she thought.

"All right, let's get started." Kristi's laptop was open and ready.

Claire sipped her latte. "First I need a timeline. After I talk to my lawyer tomorrow, I'll call my friend Brenda about listing the condo for me."

Sam tapped the eraser end of her pencil against the page on her clipboard. "Will Donald agree to using her?"

"He won't have a choice. We're co-owners, but this is my home and I want total control over how it's being shown. I trust Brenda, so Donald will have to trust her, too."

Kristi dug her calendar out of her bag and flipped it open. "Sam and I should finish up at the Fletcher house tomorrow, and I have an appointment with a prospective client on Thursday morning, otherwise my week is clear."

"I'm going to a demolition site on Wednesday to salvage some oak flooring and anything else that looks promising. Other than that, I'm all yours."

"I appreciate this so much," Claire said. "I don't think there's much we need to do here."

"I agree. Your home always looks like a magazine spread," Sam said.

Kristi looked around and gave a little sigh. "No toys, no stray items of clothing, no dog hair all over everything."

And no character, Claire thought. None whatsoever. Starting tomorrow there might be a dog, though. Maybe a baby in nine months. Her pulse sped up. She shouldn't even be thinking about that possibility, and this wasn't the time to distract her friends with those tidbits.

"And you both know how much I envy you."

"Your turn will come," Sam said.

"And when it does, you're going to be an awesome mom. And dog owner," Kristi said, because everyone knew Claire wanted one. "Now, about that timeline…"

"Right. Lawyer and real estate agent tomorrow. Our calendars are all clear on Tuesday, so we can start in here. Sam, I don't think we need much in terms of renovations, but I've always thought I could make more of the terrace."

"I agree. I'll take some measurements out there today and see what I can come up with. Right away I'm thinking cedar planters and some bench seating that includes built-in storage. Those are easy to build on-site, especially if I have the boards precut, and they can be left to age naturally."

"That's a great idea," Kristi said. "Inside I'll want to unify the look. You have some lovely folk art pieces—the welcome wreath on the door, the painted milk can you use for umbrellas. They're very homey and totally you, but the contrast between those things and the modern interior is too…contrasty."

Claire knew that, but she loved those things because to her they gave the place a cosier feel. "I'll pack them up and put them in my storage locker," she said as she typed it into her task list. "What else?"

Kristi gazed around the space. "The decor is very monochromatic. That adds to the ultramodern feel of the space, but it also feels generic so I think you should layer in some colour. We'll look for a few simple pieces that will work here and that you'll be able to take to your new place."

"And now we're talking colors." Sam stood and unclipped a measuring tape from her belt. "That's my cue to go out and take a look at the terrace. Just promise me there won't be any wallpaper."

"No wallpaper, I promise!" Claire laughed and gave her a wave. "Go do your thing. We'll come get you when we've finished in here."

LUKE WAS THE FIRST TO arrive for the meeting at the precinct. He paced across the room and back, twice, and was debating whether to stay put or go look for Kate Bradshaw to see if she'd dug up anything on Donald when Jason Wong strode into the room.

"Afternoon, Sarge."

"Luke. Glad you could make it. Where's everyone else?"

"Don't know. Maybe finishing their Sunday brunch and cursing the boss who called them before noon on a Sunday and told them to get down here for a meeting?"

Jason laughed. "Yeah, I'm a real ogre. There've been a couple new developments, including information on Phong's whereabouts. Could be the break we've been waiting for."

It was about time. "I'm sure everyone's on their way. In fact, here's one now," he said as Cam Ferguson walked into the room.

"Jason, Luke. How's it going?"

They both agreed it was going well.

"Thanks for coming in. I know you haven't had a lot of sleep."

Luke hadn't, either, but at least he'd spent the night in

a bed. After Cam had finished up at the airport yesterday, he'd taken over for Lindi in one of the surveillance vans.

Cam ran a hand over the stubble on his chin and glanced at the clock on the wall behind Jason's desk. "Couple hours."

"It shows," Luke said, knowing his colleague could take a little good-natured ribbing, no matter how sleep-deprived he was.

"Unlike Detective Smithe-with-an-*e*," Wong said as Patsy strolled in, a Starbucks cup in one hand, her phone in the other, calm, cool and collected as always.

"What can I say? A girl needs her sleep," she quipped.

Unlike Cam, Luke figured she'd look this good on no sleep.

"Where's Derek and Dex?" Patsy asked.

Jason checked his watch. "On their way."

"I'm here, I'm here," Derek said, rushing in. "Had to drop one of the boys at the soccer field. I'd've asked the wife to do it, only she took the other one to the pool for swimming practice."

A few days ago Luke would've felt sorry for the poor guy and congratulated himself on being footloose and free of family obligations. Now as he watched Derek settle onto a chair, looking a little harried, he didn't feel so smug. From the few things Derek had said about his family, Luke got the sense that he and his wife shared household and child-raising responsibilities. They were a team. There was a time when he'd have considered this couple to be just plain lucky to have found a pattern that worked, but now he knew it was more than good fortune. Derek worked at it, so did Jason. And while Luke hadn't grown up with any kind of role model for being a husband and a father, he was surrounded by them now.

"Where's Dex?" Derek asked.

"Right behind you." Lindi Dexter stood in the doorway in paint-spattered jeans and an old sweatshirt, ponytail pulled through the back of her ball cap.

"Good of you to join us," Cam said.

Lindi grinned and flipped him the bird. "Hey, I was painting my kid's bedroom. It's my day off." She was a single mom with two teenage daughters. Luke had no idea how she managed to hold it all together, but she did. Women were way better at that than most men, or so it seemed to him.

"Now that we're all here and the pleasantries are out of the way," Jason said, wasting no time getting down to business, "we have new information on Phong. A security guard spotted him at Sea-Tac last night, coming off a red-eye from Miami. We weren't even sure he was in the country, now he's right here in our backyard."

Derek rubbed his hands together. "He's as good as ours."

"Was he alone?" Patsy asked. "Or did he bring more girls with him?"

"He's too careful for that," Jason said. "He has other people doing drug drops and smuggling the girls into the country. We've been picking up communications, though. Text messages and emails with instructions for his lackeys. Cam's been able to unencrypt them, and he figures it's Phong who's sending them."

Luke gave him a congratulatory slap on the shoulder. "Nice work."

"Thanks. The messages are coming from a cell phone, and there's good reason to believe it's Phong's. The guy's extremely careful, though, and the challenge—if and when we ever do pick him up—will be to make sure he has the phone on him. If it isn't, then he'll deny he ever had one and claim he's just a victim of circumstances, in the wrong place at the wrong time."

"Yada, yada," Patsy chimed in. "Meanwhile he's smuggling girls, and by girls I mean children, into the States and forcing them into the sex trade. We need to get this guy."

"We're close," Jason said. "And getting closer by the hour. That's why I needed you all here for a face-to-face. If we're going to pull this off, we need a unified effort. Luke has a new development, and I'll start by letting him fill you in on that."

"As you know, a friend of mine lives in that condominium complex," Luke said, choosing his words carefully. Wong was aware of what was happening with him and Claire, but no one else had to.

"Fancy digs," Lindi said.

"And you say she's a friend?" Cam smirked. "That's not your usual modus operandi."

Funny. "I've known her since college. She has some personal stuff happening right now and I'm going to be staying with her a bit." He'd filled in their sergeant on all the pertinent details, including Donald's behavior, and he'd been honest and up-front when Wong asked if he was sleeping with her. The others could speculate all they wanted, but they didn't need the same level of detail. "This gives us the perfect opportunity to set up surveillance on the interior of the Phong condo. We can see everyone who comes and goes, and if he shows up, we'll know it. If we're lucky enough to see him with his phone, we go in."

"Once he's there, we won't need luck," Cam said. "I'm already set up to route some communication to his phone through a server in Vietnam. If he responds, we've got him."

"We've managed to get into an empty suite two floors down," Jason told them. "We'll have Derek and Patsy there along with a couple guys from SWAT at all times. They'll make sure we get access to the penthouse when we need it."

"So Luke's friend," Patsy said. "You've brought her in on this? Are you sure that's a good idea?"

"No, we haven't," Jason said. "Luke and I talked it over and decided against it. He's moving in this afternoon and setting up a telescope on a tripod. Pretty standard for a lot of those places. People like to check out the boats in the sound, do a little whale watching. The telescope can be swivelled around to look at anything. The camera's built into the tripod itself, so it'll be stationary and aimed at the penthouse twenty-four-seven. Cam's got his IT guys working on it right now."

Derek grinned. "Watch out, bad guys."

"We are good," Lindi said. "I could use something like that to keep an eye on my girls when I'm not around."

"See me after the meeting," Cam said to her. "I'll get you set up."

That got a laugh from everyone.

As always, Jason allowed them a moment of good-natured camaraderie before reining them in. "To summarize, we'll have Luke in the penthouse, Lindi and Cam monitoring the footage we get from the camera, and Derek and Patsy ready to move in. There's a good possibility that some of Phong's girls don't speak much English, if any. It'll be good to have a woman in there, especially one who can communicate with them. The plan is to have everything and everyone in place by early this evening. Let's hope our guy doesn't keep us waiting."

"So Luke doesn't get to swing from the side of the building on the window-washing platform?" Lindi asked.

The question had Jason grinning. "'Fraid not. Now that we have a better option in place, it's too risky. Right now, at least as far as we know, we're flying under their radar and we want to keep it that way. Phong and his boys might think it's more than a coincidence that we have a crew gawking through their windows, so I've pulled the window-washing crew off the site."

"Damn." Cam smacked his palms together. "I was looking forward to seeing him up there."

"Maybe next time," Luke said. "Or maybe you'll draw that straw."

"Me and heights?" Cam said. "No way. I can't even stand on a stepladder to change a lightbulb."

"But you're okay with it being me."

"Oh, I have no problem with that."

Luke laughed along with the others. Cam liked to give everyone a hard time but when push came to shove, he had everyone's back. Luke hadn't actually minded the assignment. After all, it's what had reconnected him with Claire. Now he had an even better vantage point, not to mention a nice big bed and a beautiful woman to share it with. Call it fate or karma or just plain luck, things could not have worked out better.

As soon as the meeting broke up, Luke assured his boss he'd be back to pick up the surveillance equipment, then excused himself and made his way out to the front desk, hoping Kate Bradshaw would be there.

His luck was holding.

"Hey, Luke. Good you're here. I have something to show you."

"Am I going to like it?" he asked.

"Not even a little bit." She opened a drawer, pulled out a folder and handed it to him.

Luke flipped it open and scanned the sheet. A couple of speeding tickets, one DUI, for which some fancy lawyer got him an acquittal, and... Shit. A restraining order filed by a former girlfriend, and one charge of sexual misconduct, brought about by an employee who later dropped the charges. Luke usually liked knowing his instincts were bang on, but this was different. If it was just Donald, yeah, he'd be smug as hell. But this was about Claire, and given the guy's behavior, any self-righteousness Luke might have indulged in was eroded by concern. The guy was a piece of work, and he'd bet anything that Claire wasn't aware of any of this.

"Thanks, Kate. I owe you one."

She grinned. "I'll add it to your tab."

"So how's it going?" he asked, figuring he owed her a little small talk after all she'd done for him. She had been paired up with him right after she graduated the academy, and they'd hit it off. He'd even toyed with the idea of asking her out, and he'd been pretty sure she would have said yes. In the end he'd decided it best not to complicate things, and now thanked his lucky stars he'd had the good sense and good judgment to keep things professional.

"Everything's going great," she said. "This is my last shift on the desk. After my days off, I'll be back on the street."

Good cops hated paperwork, so it was a positive sign that she didn't like working the desk. "Give me a shout when you're back on the job. If our investigation is still ongoing—" Although he hoped to God it would be wrapped by then. He was ready for something new, and he hated the idea of deceiving Claire any longer than absolutely necessary. "If it is, I'll talk to Wong about finding a place for you. If not on this op, then maybe the next."

Her eyes brightened, exactly the reaction he was looking for. "Really? Thanks, Luke. That'd be great."

"Happy to do it." He folded the report she'd printed for him, stuck it in his back pocket and handed the file folder back to her. "Thanks again for this."

He didn't like most of what was in it, but he was more certain than ever that being at Claire's was the right place to be. He'd be a happy man once the investigation wrapped up and he could come clean about one of his reasons for wanting to be there. Meanwhile they would deal with Donald. And maybe, just maybe, Luke and Claire would figure out where this thing between them was going. He still didn't know exactly how he felt about her, but he damn sure wanted to stick around and figure it out.

Chapter Nine

It took Claire and Kristi less than half an hour to do a quick tour of the apartment, take photographs and make notes. They decided to use a vibrant shade of cranberry for their accent color, and settled on a time on Tuesday afternoon to shop for accessories.

"A few pillows, a vase, some nice tall tapers in those silver candlesticks," Kristi said. "It'll be perfect."

"It will," Claire agreed. "Thank you for this. I'm so bad at this sort of thing."

"That's why you have me." Kristi gave her a hug. "Let's go see what Sam's up to. I'm ready to wrap up the work portion of the program and get on to the fun stuff."

Claire had to admit that she was looking forward to it, too. She passed around bottled water from the fridge after they regrouped around the table, took a seat and turned her iPad back on.

"I know you have a bunch of questions about Luke." They would no doubt have some questionable suggestions, too. "But first I have something to show you. Yesterday morning, before I met my new clients, I spent some time at the office searching the listings, and I think I found a house."

"Claire! You've been holding out on us!"

"Let's see it!"

She brought it up on the screen. "Here it is." She gazed at the listing, even more certain than the last time she looked at it, that this was it. This was home. She held her breath as she angled the screen so her friends could see it.

Kristi's eyes lit up. "Oh, sweetie. It's adorable. It even has a white picket fence, and I love the bay window. Is that the living room?"

"It must be, at least I hope it is. I've always wanted a living room with a bay window. It'll be perfect for a Christmas tree. And the house is bigger than it looks from the street. There are three bedrooms, plus it has an eat-in kitchen as well as a formal dining room."

"Have you looked at it already?"

"Not yet. I was hoping the two of you would look at it with me."

Kristi clapped her hands excitedly.

Claire turned to Sam, who had yet to say anything. "What do you think?"

"I think it's perfect for you. I was planning to build you a white picket fence for a housewarming present. Now I'll have to come up with something else."

"That's so sweet. I have to confess that I did a drive-by on my way home yesterday and the fence looks as though it could use some work and a fresh coat of paint."

"Consider it done. Does it have a second story or is this upper window in the attic?"

"The listing says it's one floor with a crawlspace, so I guess it must be an attic."

"I'll take a stepladder when we go to see it. I'd like to take a look up there. The roof appears to be in good shape, but we still want to be sure the attic's dry and insulated."

"And I'll take lots of interior photos so we can work on the design."

"If I decide to put in an offer." Was this crazy? Was she

crazy? She hated change. She never did anything without making a list, setting up a spreadsheet, looking at all the angles, weighing all the pros and cons.

And look at you now.

In fewer than forty-eight hours she had decided to go ahead with the divorce and sell the condo. She had rushed into an affair with a man who was, by his own admission, not relationship material. At least, not as far as she was concerned. He didn't want a family, *not ever,* and she wanted one more than anything. She'd had sex without taking the proper precautions and there was a chance she could be pregnant. Now she was seriously thinking about putting an offer on a house she hadn't even seen, and she was already daydreaming about turning one of the bedrooms into a nursery.

"Oh, no," Kristi said. "No, no, no, no. Don't start, don't you dare."

"What?"

"You're having second thoughts."

"No, I'm not."

"Yes, you are." Sam leaned across the table and grabbed her hand. "You've got your I'm-having-serious-second-thoughts face on, and it isn't pretty."

Kristi took her other hand and squeezed. "Sam's right. You have to do this for yourself, hon. Dive in headfirst without thinking about it."

She'd already done more than her share of leaping without looking this weekend, but they were right. This was something she had to do for herself. Not because Donald was demanding she do it, and definitely not because she secretly hoped there could be a future in this thing, whatever it was, with Luke.

"I know, and I will. I probably should have done this a long time ago."

"You needed to do it when you were ready," Sam said.

"And now that you are," Kristi said, "we're with you, every step of the way."

"Thanks, guys. I don't know what I'd do without you." She was the steady one, the one with both feet firmly planted, the giver of advice. Being on the receiving end was new, and she had a feeling she'd better get used to it.

"Soo," Kristi said. "You and Luke. I can't believe you never told us about him."

"Or how, after someone like him, you somehow ended up with Donald."

"Sam!" Kristi's admonishment was quick, and unconvincing.

"I'm sorry. I never liked him, and there's no sense pretending I did."

"It's okay, Sam. I don't like him anymore, either. But Luke and I were never…you know. We were just friends."

"Right. Just *friends*." Kristi laughed. "In case you're wondering," she said, winking at Sam, "that's what we called it when we were in college."

"I see. I went to trade school. We didn't have any fancy euphemisms for hooking up."

"No, we really were just friends, and we did not hook up. Believe it or not, we used to study together."

"Seriously? If I'd had a study partner like him, I never would have been able to concentrate. I would have flunked out for sure."

Claire had been too much of a Goody Two-shoes to let anything like that happen, but she had surreptitiously studied Luke over the top of a textbook on plenty of occasions, and yes, she'd been distracted more than once.

"We don't really care about the past anyway," Sam said. "Not when the present is so much more…" She paused and feigned a dreamy-eyed pose.

"Yummy," Kristi said, filling in the blank. "Where did you run in to him?"

"Just down the street, in front of the next building. He was—" Best not to mention the window-washing thing, she decided. "I'm not sure what he was doing. Some sort of police work, I guess."

"Oooh, was he in uniform?" Kristi's expression matched Sam's.

"No. He's a detective, undercover and all that, so he doesn't seem to wear one."

"And then he got under your covers," Sam said, waggling her eyebrows.

"Seriously?" Claire asked. "You couldn't let that one go this time?"

"Not a chance, not even a slim one." Sam, pencil tucked behind one ear, sipped some water from her bottle.

"Where do you think this is going?" Kristi asked. "Or is it too soon to tell?"

Definitely not too soon to know it was going nowhere. Luke had made it clear that he wasn't relationship material and he really wasn't daddy material. He had been completely up-front about it, and for her, for now, that was okay.

"Not too soon at all. He's not a family man, and right now I'm not looking for one. I'm still trying to undo one mistake and I'm not about to make another. Luke is fun to be with—"

"I'll bet he is." Sam grinned, and there went those eyebrows again.

Kristi put an arm around Claire's shoulders, gave them an affectionate squeeze. "If anyone deserves to have some fun, it's you. What about Donald? How's he taking this?"

Claire shrugged. "I'm sure he doesn't care, but he is getting on my case about the divorce, and about selling the condo, and about getting his hands on the book his grandmother gave me."

"I can understand why he'd want to get his money out of the condo. I'm not saying that justifies him harassing you," Kristi was quick to add. "Just that I get it. What I don't get is why he'd want an old children's book. That seems totally out of character."

Claire had thought so, too. "I agree, or at least I did until I went online and did a little research. I took the book to the office yesterday, in case Donald decides to come here to look for it."

Sam's eyes widened. "I never thought of that. You need to change the locks."

"I did." She just didn't want to explain what had prompted that. "Anyway, I did a quick search for the book his grandmother gave me. It's an old edition of Beatrix Potter's *The Tale of Peter Rabbit,* and it turns out to be worth a lot of money."

"A kid's book?" Sam asked.

"How much is a lot?" Kristi asked.

"Thousands of dollars."

"Wow!"

"Really?"

"I was surprised, too, but that explains why Donald wants it."

"I thought he was loaded," Sam said.

Claire shrugged. "He earns a good salary but he likes to spend money as much as he likes to make it, and if his investments aren't doing well, he could be having some cash-flow problems."

"I can't tell you how relieved I am to know you've changed the lock," Kristi said. "We've both been worried about you. It was a good idea to have Sam at your open house yesterday, too, and I want you to promise to keep us in the loop. If he's harassing you or, God forbid, worse, you need to tell us."

"And tell Luke," Sam added. "Donald hasn't got the balls to mess with him."

She was so right, Claire thought. Recalling the look on Donald's face after his unexpected appearance on Friday night, and Luke's very unexpected reaction, still made her want to giggle.

Sam checked her watch and jumped up. "I have to get going. The nanny is off today and AJ's holding down the fort."

Kristi did the same. "Me, too. Nate took the girls to the mall, and in exchange I told him I'd walk the dogs when I get home. You'll let us know when you'd like to look at the house?"

"Of course."

"And you'll call if Donald gives you any more grief?"

"I'll call, I promise."

Before they left, she hugged them both and again congratulated Sam on the baby news. She felt guilty for not being completely open and honest with them about Donald's recent antics, but nothing would be gained by it and they would worry unnecessarily.

She closed the door, locked it and leaned against it. Donald was Donald. He could be a jerk, but he wasn't dangerous. Was he?

LUKE DROPPED HIS DUFFEL bag to the floor outside Claire's door, leaned the case containing the telescope against the wall and studied the Home Sweet Home wreath that made, now that he thought about it, an odd statement about the reality on the other side of the door. More like wishful thinking on Claire's part. He wanted to see her, had looked forward to this moment since he'd left for his meeting late that morning, but he couldn't bring himself to slide the key into the lock. He hated to deceive her, not tell her that he had more than one reason for wanting to be with her.

Given his track record with women, that realization caught him off guard. Had he ever been completely open with a woman? Or been willing to acknowledge the true depth of his feelings? No. But then he'd never felt like this before, and he didn't know why. Could be that in the past the booze had taken the edge off his conscience. Or it could have something to do with the woman waiting for him on the other side of this door. Easier to believe this was about being sober than it was to sort out his feelings for Claire. Whatever it was, he couldn't stand here all night, holding on to a piece of brass he was reluctant to use.

"What do you think, Rex? Ready to go inside?"

The dog had been waiting patiently next to the duffel bag since Luke had given him the command to sit. He remained sitting, although his tail wagged in response to the question.

"You might not be so chipper after you meet Chloe."

Rex cocked his head to one side.

"Did I forget to mention her?"

The dog's head tipped to the other side.

"Sorry, buddy." He stuck the key in the lock and turned it. "You'll figure out a way to get along with her. Besides, we can't stand out here all night."

The scent of something cooking greeted him as he opened the door. Garlic, oregano…pasta sauce would be his guess. He hadn't realized how hungry he was. And then Claire joined him in the foyer and suddenly he was a different kind of hungry.

Without hesitation she glided up to him, slid an arm around his waist, tipped her head back for a kiss. Her lips were soft and inviting, the kiss full of promise. Too bad his hands were already full, or he'd be tempted to explore the shapely curves of the black dress that was primly covered by a red-and-white checked apron.

"Something smells good. Besides you, that is."

"Lasagna."

"Homemade?"

"Mmm-hmm." She pulled him in for one more kiss. "It's one of my favorite things."

"Mine, too."

"Do you need a hand with—" She stepped back and her eyes lit up. "Rex! I was hoping you'd bring him. What a handsome boy you are." She petted the top of Rex's head, and he opened his mouth and started to pant.

"I bought dog biscuits for him. Is it okay to give him one now?"

"Sure."

"I was hoping you'd say yes." She pulled a treat from her apron pocket.

"Sit," Luke said.

Knowing what was in store, Rex readily complied.

"Good dog." Claire offered the biscuit and Rex gingerly took it. "He's a beautiful dog, Luke. I'm glad you brought him with you. Do you need a hand with the rest of your things?"

"Thanks, I can manage." He set his duffel bag on the foyer floor and reached back into the hallway for the telescope.

"That's everything?" Claire asked.

"This is it. For now. I can always run back to my place if I need anything."

"What about Rex's food?"

He toed the duffel. "It's in here."

"And the box?"

"Oh, ah, that's a telescope. I hope you don't mind. Since

you have such a great view, I thought I'd set up it over there." He indicated the long stretch of windows in the living room. "Check out the harbor, that kind of thing."

Claire smiled. "Good idea. Donald used to keep binoculars in there, but a telescope sounds even better. For now, why don't you put the dog food in the kitchen and take your things down to the bedroom while I finish dinner?"

"Sure thing."

It was all very domestic, and yet it no longer felt right. Jason Wong had emphasized the importance of not letting Claire in on Luke's reason for being here. And much as he tried to tell himself that he was there for her, to make sure Donald didn't give her any more grief, there was no denying that his primary reason for moving in was to follow through with this investigation. To do that, he had to deceive her. There was no getting around it, and there was no denying it.

The cat was curled up asleep on the end of the bed. She got up, stretched, yawned and blinked at him when he came into the room, and responded favorably when he scratched the back of her neck.

"You might not like me so much when you see who I've brought with me."

He left the cat licking her paws and grooming her ears and went to join Claire and Rex in the kitchen. The dog sat on the floor next to her, hoping for another treat.

"Rex. Over here." Luke pointed to a floor mat.

The dog slunk over and sprawled on it.

"Good boy. Stay."

Claire was standing at the island, tossing a salad. "He sure is well-behaved."

"He was well-trained when I got him. The trick is to not let up with it. He knows the limits, and he lives for the rewards."

"Like dog biscuits?"

"Mostly it's going for a run every day, fetching his rope toy, hanging out at the dog park."

"Nice life, Rex," Claire said with a smile. "It's a little cooler tonight so I thought we'd eat inside. Is that okay with you?"

"Sounds good. I'll set up my telescope, unless you'd like help with dinner?"

"Go ahead. I have everything under control."

The setup for the telescope/webcam was every bit as easy as the techies had assured him it would be. And for several minutes, since Claire was watching from the kitchen, he made a pretext of actually looking at a couple of boats anchored out in the sound. He would have to remember to do that from time to time so she didn't get suspicious.

Finally he settled on a stool across the counter from her, which was really where he wanted to be.

"I have sparkling water if you'd like some."

"Sure."

"Ice?" she asked. "Lime?"

"Both, thanks."

From a black lacquered tray at the end of the island, she scooped cubes from a silver ice bucket into tall glasses, filled them and slid a slice of lime onto the rim of each glass.

She passed one across to him and started on a salad dressing, measuring olive oil, balsamic and herbs into a bowl, whisking them together.

"I figured you didn't like to cook." He added the lime to the water in his glass and took a long drink.

"Seriously? What made you think that?"

"There wasn't much in your fridge that first morning."

She set the salad dressing aside and reached for her

glass. "The only thing I like more than cooking is eating. I've been trying to diet, so having a lot of food around is way too tempting."

Again, he wanted to say she didn't need to worry about her weight, and once more decided against it. "I know all about temptation," he said instead.

"I know you do."

He liked that when the subject of alcohol came up, she didn't pussyfoot around.

"For me it's dessert, especially anything chocolate. The darker and richer, the better. Although…" She hesitated, as though not sure she wanted to expand on that. "I've also been known to sit and watch a movie and polish off an entire bag of cookies."

Somehow that didn't sound as bad as an evening spent with a bottle of whiskey, even though she seemed to think it did. "Everything in moderation is never as easy as it sounds."

"Tell me about it. Anyway, I do love to cook, and it was fun to shop this afternoon after Sam and Kristi left, knowing there'd be someone here to cook for."

"You went out after your meeting this afternoon?" He wanted it to sound like a casual question, but the police report Kate had given him earlier was still burning a hole in his back pocket.

The look she gave him was easily just as scorching. "Yes, I did. I can't hide, always have someone here with me, never go out on my own. Yes, Donald's making a nuisance of himself, and yes, I wish he would stop, but he won't hurt me."

Let it go. Sharing the details of that report with her now would ruin their evening. In the morning he'd find a way to bring up Donald's checkered past without letting her know he'd actually seen the report. Bringing it here had been a dumb move. He should have left it at his apartment when he'd picked up Rex.

"How'd the meeting go with your business partners?" he asked.

The timer went, and as she pulled a pan of lasagna from the oven and served it onto plates, she excitedly shared the details for staging her condo before putting it on the market, and the plan to look at a new place on Tuesday.

He carried the plates to the dining table that was already set with candles, cutlery and cloth napkins, and Claire followed with the salad.

Rex stood up, as though expecting an invitation to join them.

"Stay."

Rex's disappointment was palpable.

"Would he like to go out on the terrace?" Claire asked. "It's not quite the same as having a backyard, but it might be more interesting for him than sitting on a mat."

Before either of them could get up to open the double doors, Claire's cat strolled into the room. She took one look at the dog and arched herself into a pose perfect for Halloween, ears back, hackles raised. Rex dropped to the floor, flattened himself on the mat and crossed his paws over his nose.

"That is too funny," Claire said, laughing at the pair of them. "In spite of Chloe's hissy fits every time she sees a dog, I don't think she'd ever actually go near one. And poor Rex doesn't seem to realize he's way bigger and tougher than she is."

"That's why he didn't make the K-9 unit. He's a good tracker but every time he sees a cat, he drops like a rock."

"I wonder why."

"We figure he must've had a run-in with a cat when he was a pup, but no one knows for sure. He's a good dog, otherwise. Smart, dependable, fearless, except when it comes to cats."

Claire got up from the table and opened the terrace doors. "Want to go outside, Rex? She won't bother you out there."

"Go," Luke said.

Rex leapt to his feet and made a run for it.

"Chloe doesn't go outside?" Luke asked.

Claire came back to the table and sat down. "Not a chance. She's pretty much afraid of her own shadow. Her reaction to dogs is purely a defense mechanism."

Luke picked up his fork and sampled the lasagna. "Wow, this is really good."

"Thank you."

"Seriously, this is probably the best I've ever tasted. Where'd you learn to cook like this?"

"From my Nonna DeAngelo. My sister and I used to spend summer vacations with her in Chicago. She's an amazing cook, and lasagna is one of her specialties. I like to think mine is almost as good as hers."

"Hard to imagine anything better than this," he said after downing another mouthful.

Claire wagged a finger at him. "If you ever meet my nonna, it'll be best not to mention that."

He had just been starting to relax, getting used to the idea of being here with Claire, but the thought of meeting her family brought back the guilt he'd been feeling while he stood outside her door a while ago. He wanted to be here with her, regretted that he had to deceive her, hated to think how she'd react when she found out.

Maybe she didn't need to find out.

That was always a possibility, one the old Luke would have welcomed and taken full advantage of. The man he was now, the man he wanted to be with Claire, couldn't do it. He needed to prove to her that he was honest, reliable and here for her, so that by the time they busted the brothel and, hopefully, had Phong in custody, she wouldn't feel she'd been taken advantage of.

He'd start by cleaning up the kitchen. And then he'd take her down the hall and remind her again why she really needed him here.

Chapter Ten

Driving home from the office late Friday afternoon gave Claire a chance to reflect on all the changes in her life since she had run into Luke. So many changes that it was nearly impossible to believe it had only been a week ago. The days since Luke moved in had flown by in a flurry of appointments with her lawyer, her real estate agent and her business partners. Those were interspersed with moments spent with him, some stolen, others planned, all like a dream that had unexpectedly yet almost magically come true.

His dog and her cat had grudgingly reached a truce, although Rex was still on the defensive whenever Chloe got too close. Claire loved taking Rex for a walk, and one afternoon she had even gone for a run with him and Luke. Just as suspected, she'd had a hard time keeping up.

Twice Luke had taken her out on the Ducati, and she'd decided that living dangerously had some serious advantages. The only thing better than riding on the bike, with her arms around him and her body on fire, happened in the bedroom.

What struck her most, though, was how much he had changed over the years. Sitting astride the bike in his leather jacket, he still looked very much like the devilish Luke Devlin she'd crushed on in college, but the reality was very much the opposite. He was thoughtful about how he adapted to her routine, interested in her ideas and opinions on everything, helpful around the house. A gentleman in every sense of the word. Every woman's fantasy. The bedroom was another matter. Her fantasy was no match for the reality, and he wanted to be with her, Claire De-Angelo, in spite of the extra pounds.

On Monday she'd met with her lawyer and gone over the divorce papers, and they had pretty much agreed with everything. There would be a fifty-fifty split of the proceeds of the condominium after it sold. To her relief, Donald wasn't asking for anything from her business, which meant she couldn't go after any of his investments, either. Since she wanted nothing of his, that was not a problem. The only sticking point was the Beatrix Potter book, and now that she knew its value and that he would sell it the first chance he got, she had dug in her heels and flatly refused to hand it over.

Still tucked inside the book was the card his grandmother had written when she had given the book to her.

Dearest Claire,

Because you share my love of books, I'm giving this one to you. It's my hope that someday you'll share *The Tale of Peter Rabbit* with your children, and so they learn the importance of always listening to their mother.

With much love,
Hettie Robinson

She had shown the card to her lawyer, who agreed that the book had undisputedly been a gift to Claire, not to

Claire and Donald. She was confident that, if necessary, a judge would agree, so the book was removed from the property settlement and for now remained locked in the safe at the Ready Set Sold office. On Kristi's suggestion, as they staged the condo, the rest of Claire's collection of children's books had been packed into boxes, three of them, and hauled down to the storage room.

Luke had helped her, and he had been surprised by how many she had and how old some of them were. Many had been hers since childhood—several even contained her name awkwardly printed in crayon. Others she'd acquired over the years at bookstores, flea markets and garage sales, and a few had been gifts from close friends who knew about her passion for children's books.

Luke had also seemed taken aback by her fondness for them. She hadn't wanted to ask why, but she could guess. To him they likely represented the things he didn't want, including a family.

With everything that had happened this week, Claire had pushed the possibility of a pregnancy to the back of her mind. Now, driving home at the end of a busy week and looking forward to some free time this weekend, all the what-ifs and the flutter of anxiety that accompanied them were back.

Don't think about it. It was probably still too soon for a home pregnancy test to give reliable results, and she wasn't sure she wanted to know anyway. Right now, by not knowing, she didn't owe Luke any kind of explanation. If she was pregnant, she would have to tell him, and she didn't know how he would react.

Yes, you do.

He would react to her news the same way he reacted to Sherri's. Badly. He'd feel duped and angry, and who could blame him? She'd told him she was on the Pill, and he'd had sex with her, believing she had everything taken care of. She'd gone into this knowing it wasn't a forever thing but she was happy right now, maybe happier than she had ever been, and she wasn't ready for it to end.

She debated whether or not to stop and pick up groceries, and decided against it. She was in a celebratory mood, and she and Luke deserved a night out. Yesterday she'd put the condominium on the market, and this morning she had put an offer on the little yellow house with the white picket fence. It was a good offer, and her agent expected a response from the sellers by this evening. The house was perfect, and she had her fingers crossed she would get the response she was hoping for. As soon as she got home, she would call to make a reservation at her favorite Italian restaurant, then she'd run a nice hot bubble bath. If Luke was home, maybe he'd join her.

Her body was already humming with anticipation as she turned the corner onto her street and saw the police barricade at the end of the block, in front of her building.

No, it was the building next door.

That's where Luke had been doing some sort of undercover work with a window-washing company, although, come to think of it, he hadn't mentioned it again and she hadn't seen them there this week.

A uniformed officer waved her around the corner, which meant she couldn't access the underground parking garage. She rolled down her car window.

"Hi," she said to the man in the middle of the intersection. "I live in this building."

"Sorry, ma'am. The street's closed due to a police incident. I can't let anyone through."

"You mean I can't get into my apartment?"

"I'm afraid not."

"Do you know what this is about, or how long it's going

to last?" It was obviously something pretty serious, but she couldn't help feeling a little resentful. There was a bubble bath up there that had her name on it.

"Sorry," he said. An unintelligible voice crackled over his radio, although apparently he understood it because he gave a clipped response before turning his attention back to her. "Ma'am, I have to ask you to move along. We need to keep this area clear for emergency vehicles."

This was getting her nowhere. Better to find a place to park and call Luke. Maybe he could get her inside.

Two blocks away she pulled into a parking space, dug her phone out of her bag and pulled up Luke's number. The call went to voice mail, so she gathered her handbag and briefcase from the passenger seat and walked the two blocks downhill to her building. Since this was a police matter, Luke had to be here. If she could find him, he could tell her what was going on, maybe even get her inside.

The police officer she'd spoken to earlier was occupied with more motorists wanting to know what was going on. Beyond the barricade were numerous police cars with lights flashing, two ambulances and dozens of people milling around on the sidewalk across the street. On the corner, a news reporter she recognized from a local television station faced a camera and spoke into a microphone, but Claire couldn't get close enough to hear what she was saying.

She scanned the crowd, looking for Luke and hoping she didn't find Donald. After they'd listed the condo and her lawyer had sent the amended divorce papers to his lawyer, he had backed off this week. Now would not be a good time for him to show up.

What on earth was going on here? she wondered as she continued her search for Luke. And then there he was, lean and solid, dark hair curling over the collar of his leather jacket. She'd recognize that jacket anywhere. He stood with his back to her, talking with two other men, Rex sitting at his side. They were almost as tall as Luke. The one facing her had sandy-blond hair and was wearing a grey Seahawks hooded sweatshirt. The other had jet-black hair and a faded jean jacket. Both were undercover cops like Luke, she was sure of it. Whatever this was, it must be big.

After a quick backward glance to see that the officer on the street was still distracted by onlookers and passersby, she slipped past the barricade, dodging other people as she made her way toward him. She was within earshot when the blond guy in the grey hoodie reached out and gave Luke a playful jab in the shoulder.

"Nice work, Luke. If you hadn't sweet-talked that chick upstairs into letting you move in and set up surveillance, we'd've never have nailed this guy."

"And you managed to keep her in the dark all this time?" the dark-haired guy asked.

Luke nodded and laughed. "She doesn't have a clue."

Several seconds ticked by before she realized they were talking about her, and then her shoes might as well have been glued to the pavement. Luke had laughed. Called her...

"Clueless?" She must have said it out loud because three heads swung her way.

Luke's cocky grin faded as the color literally drained from his face.

She had let herself be taken in by his looks, his charms, all that phoney vulnerability. What had seemed too good to be true was, well, too good to be true. She had acted like a fool, and he had played her as one.

"You smug son of a bitch. You *sweet-talked* me into this? You think I'm *clueless?*"

"Shit. Claire, listen—"

"No, *you* listen. As soon as this three-ring circus is cleared up, I want you and your crap out of my apartment."

"I can explain—"

"Explain what? That you still treat women the way you always did, sweet-talking them into giving you whatever you want? Save your breath. I get it. You haven't changed at all."

The touch of Rex's cool, damp nose against her hand tugged at her heartstrings, but not enough to calm her down. She should be furious, but right now the humiliation left no room for anger. She had nothing to say, and she'd be stupid to stand here and let him make this even worse, so she did the only thing that made sense. She swung away from him and ran.

After no more than ten steps he caught up and grabbed her by the arm. "Claire, wait."

"No!" She pulled away. "Don't touch me."

He let go immediately. "I know how that sounded but if you'd let me explain—"

No way. "I might be naive, but I'm not stupid." Aware of the people around them, that his friends were watching, she struggled to keep calm. "The sweet talk is over, Luke. We're done." She turned away again and this time he let her go.

She hurried past the barricade and up the hill to her car. After the first block, she stopped to catch her breath and glanced back to be sure he wasn't following her. He wasn't.

She trudged up the second block, cursing men for being heartless, heartbreaking jerks, cursing Seattle's steep hills, wondering what she should do when she did get to her car. Call one of her friends? Kristi, she decided. She was good in a crisis.

Once in her car, she locked the doors and pulled a bottle of water out of her bag. Her hands shook so bad, it was all she could do to unscrew the cap and hold the bottle to her lips long enough to take a few sips. After she put it away and drew a couple of deep breaths, she got out her phone and called Kristi.

"Oh, sweetie. I'm so sorry," her friend said after Claire spilled the details. "You need to come straight to my place, as long as you're okay to drive. I can pick you up if you'd like."

"I'm okay." Or at least better than she'd been a few minutes ago. "Thanks, Kristi."

"Don't even mention it. I'm pretty sure I owe you one anyway. I'll call Sam and see if she's free. She'll either join us, or go hunt Luke down and kick his ass."

That made Claire laugh. "See, this is why I love you guys."

"Right back at you. Now get yourself over here."

"I'm on my way." She tossed the phone into her bag and pulled on her sunglasses. She hoped Kristi would let her stay the night. She had no idea when she could get back into her building, and she wouldn't go back, anyway. Not until she was sure Luke had cleared out of her apartment and out of her life, this time for good.

LUKE WANTED TO PUNCH something. Of all the crappy bad luck that had come his way, this was the crappiest.

"Look, man." Cam Ferguson wore the concerned look of a man who figured he could end up on the receiving end of somebody's fist. "I am so sorry. I had no idea that was your woman."

"Not your fault." Much as Luke would like it to be. He'd been trying to play it cool, not wanting to let on to anyone that he had feelings for Claire, and it had backfired. Big-time.

"You want to go after her?" Jason asked. "We're winding down here. Patsy's already got the girls in the van. She's taking them to a safe house for questioning. And here's Derek now."

"Thanks, but I'm not sure that's a good idea."

Instead he turned his attention to the main entrance and watched Derek escort Phong, hands cuffed behind him, into the back of a waiting police car. The moment they'd all been working and waiting for, and now it was a total anticlimax. Behind them, uniformed officers led three more men out of the building. One was Phong's pimp/drug dealer. The other two were a couple of johns who had the dirty rotten luck of being in the wrong place at the wrong time.

He could relate. Before Claire showed up, he'd been about to take Rex back upstairs to the condo. Instead he'd stuck around, not wanting to miss this, and now he'd screwed up everything.

He knew Claire well enough to know that when she told him to get out, she meant it. And who could blame her? He had hurt her and he hated himself for it. Now it was up to him to find a way back in. If he wanted any kind of a shot at fixing this, he had to give her some space, a chance to calm down. It would be better to call her. Not that she would answer, but he could leave a message, apologize, explain why he couldn't be honest with her, and why he hadn't been honest with his colleagues. Could he convince her that using her place for surveillance wasn't his only reason for wanting to be with her? Or would she always believe he was still the same smug son of a bitch she'd known in college? Time would tell. All he could do now was hope for the best.

STILL HIDING BEHIND her sunglasses, Claire rang the doorbell at Kristi and Nate's place. She hoped her friend would answer the door and not her husband, her teenage daughter or her twin stepdaughters. Claire couldn't face anyone else right now. Bad enough that Kristi had to be the one to witness her meltdown. Luckily it was Kristi who opened the door because *meltdown* was a little bit of an understatement.

"Oh, sweetie. I'm so sorry." Kristi hugged her. "Come in, come in."

Claire pulled off her sunglasses and dabbed at her eyes with a tissue. It would be easy to let herself have a good cry, but she was still too furious for that.

"Come with me." Kristi led her down to the bathroom, got out fresh towels and a washcloth. "Take your time, wash your face, I'll go find you something comfortable to put on. Oh, Sam's on her way. She should be here any minute."

"What about your family…?"

"Not to worry. Jenna's at a sleepover at a friend's place, and Nate took the twins and the dogs over to his mom and dad's for the evening. We have the place all to ourselves."

That was something of a relief. It was one thing to let her two best friends see her like this, but she couldn't cope with anyone else right now.

She splashed some water on her face, ran a comb through her hair and changed into a pair of sweatpants and a T-shirt that Kristi had produced. There was no way Kristi's clothes would fit her so these must be Nate's, but she was beyond caring.

In the family room, she found that Sam had arrived.

"Come sit here," she said, patting the sofa seat cushion next to her.

"I'll go fix us some drinks." Kristi urged her to take a seat. "Be right back."

Claire sat and sank into Sam's embrace, and Sam plucked a tissue from the box and pressed it into her hand.

"Thanks." She had never been a crier, though. It didn't solve anything anyway. It was just that this hurt so darned much.

"Kristi gave me the *Reader's Digest* version of what happened with Luke. I had already seen the TV news coverage about the place they busted and the arrests, but I never put two and two together to come up with Luke using your place for whatever kind of surveillance they were doing."

Surveillance. That's what Luke was doing, using her place, using *her*. "I honestly had no idea." She was that big a fool.

Sam filled her in on the sordid details of the young women who'd been smuggled into the country and forced into the sex trade, the drugs and how it had been the overdose and death of one of the young women several weeks ago that tipped off the police and launched the investigation.

"So it was…what? A brothel? Seriously? In my condominium complex?" Claire groaned. "And just after I've listed it. Who's going to buy it now?"

Her life was turning into a vortex and she was watching it all being sucked down the sewer. What else could go wrong?

Her phone rang. "La Cucaracha" played.

Sam snatched the phone out of her hand. "No freaking way is that loser getting to you now. Just ignore him."

"He's probably heard the news and I'll bet he's thinking the same I am, that between this and the current state of the real estate market, we'll never a find a buyer."

"Too bad," Sam said. "There's not a damn thing you can do about any of it, but he'll try to pin it all on you anyway."

That did sound like Donald. *At least he's predictable.*
Luke had been full of surprises since the moment they'd
met, and she'd had enough surprises to last a lifetime.

Kristi returned with a tray of drinks. "Sam, that's decaf
coffee for you. Claire, I was going to make you a latte, then
I decided something stronger was in order. Have a few
sips of this," she said, pressing a glass into Claire's hand.

Absently Claire gazed at the amber-colored fluid in the
cut-crystal old-fashioned glass, heard the clink of ice as
she raised it to her lips. She quickly lowered it when the
sharp, peaty scent filled her nose.

"What is this?"

"Scotch, on the rocks. It'll take the edge off."

Claire set the glass on the coffee table. "I can't drink
that."

Sam picked up her coffee cup. "We know you're not
much of a drinker, but this is one of those times when you
can make an exception."

"No, I mean I *really* can't drink that." Her current reality was all but forgotten in the face of Luke's betrayal. A
simple glass of Scotch had it rushing back.

"Why not?"

"There's no harm in one little drink."

Claire felt herself smile, and then she started to laugh.
This is so not funny, she told herself.

"Okay, now she's getting hysterical," Sam said. "What
do we do?"

"I'm not." She took a long, slow breath to calm herself.
"Honest. I don't know why I'm laughing. I'm not hysterical. I'm not. But I… There's a chance I could be pregnant."

Chapter Eleven

"Pregnant?" Sam and Kristi chorused.

"Are you sure?" Kristi swept the glass of Scotch off the table and set it on the tray.

"Is it Luke's?" Sam asked.

"No, I'm not sure. And, yes! If I'm having a baby, of course it's his. How many men do you think I've been sleeping with?"

"Sorry, sorry, sorry." Sam was obviously chagrined. "That was a stupid question. It's just… Oh, my God, I was not expecting this."

"How did this happen?" Kristi asked. "I mean, I know how it happened, but I thought you were still on the Pill."

"I am, or I was, but I missed a few, quite a few, actually." She told them how she had messed up and about the birth control her doctor had recommended until she knew for sure.

"Have you taken a pregnancy test?"

"Not yet. It's only been a week and—" This was the hardest part of her confession. "Things were going so well with Luke and I didn't want to spoil it. Even before what happened this afternoon, I knew this wasn't a forever thing. He doesn't want a family, isn't interested in settling down, and he was completely up-front about that."

But she never would have suspected he was using her. The old Luke, sure, but this Luke? Never.

"Claire, this doesn't sound like you." Kristi's narrow-eyed scrutiny made her squirm. "Did you just plan to end things at some point and have his baby without telling him?"

"Of course not! I would never do anything like that. The thing is, even though I knew he doesn't want a family, I did believe he wanted to be with me."

He had been very convincing, and she had fallen for it. Thud. Knowing how gullible she'd been, how easy it had been for him to manipulate her, hurt every bit as much as his betrayal.

"I guess I was secretly hoping his feelings were strong enough that he would change his mind. Now that I know that's not true, I'm not sure how I'll handle it." If anything needed to be handled.

"I don't know that I agree," Sam said. "When we met Luke last Sunday afternoon, I saw how he looked at you. Seriously, the guy could not take his eyes off you. It's damn hard to fake that kind of thing. Most men aren't good enough actors to pull it off."

Claire laughed, and even to her own ears it had a bitter edge to it. "Trust me, he's had a lot of practice. He had a string of girlfriends in college, and they all believed he was crazy about them...until they found out he wasn't."

"There's a difference between reality and wishful thinking," Kristi said. "I know what Sam means. The way Luke looked at you—"

Claire stopped her. "Please, stop. You both mean well and you don't want to see me hurting...I love you for that... but the thing Luke and I had, whatever it was, it's over."

"Okay, fair enough." But Sam's concession was short-lived. "I have no trouble believing the guy was a player.

I'll bet girls have been throwing themselves at him since he hit puberty. But the baby…that's a whole different matter. I'll go out on a limb here and predict he has a change of heart after you tell him."

Of course Sam would believe that. Her husband would move heaven and earth to be with his kids.

"I want to believe that as much as you do, sweetie, but I'm afraid it's not going to happen. That first morning over breakfast, Luke told me about his ex, how he'd only found out she was having his baby after she was in a car accident and had a miscarriage."

"What did he do?"

"He ended the relationship."

Sam and Kristi exchanged a look.

"Can I ask one more question?" Kristi asked.

"Of course."

"Are you in love with him?"

Claire inhaled slowly, then exhaled with a whoosh. She had doubts about a lot of things right now, but she was absolutely certain about this. "Totally, madly, head-over-heels."

"You should tell him," Sam said.

"Right. Because I haven't been humiliated enough already."

"No. Because if I'm right and he is as crazy about you as I think he is, then—"

Claire's phone went off again, this time vibrating on the coffee table where Sam had set it. Speak of the devil…

Sam picked it up, read the display name and grinned at Kristi.

"Don't answer it!" Claire said.

"It says…" Sam paused. "Lucky Devil?"

"Luke put that in my phone. I can't talk to him. Not right now." She didn't bother trying to hide the bitterness.

"He's had that stupid nickname since college. It's what his buddies called him, given his way with women." He even had the T-shirt to prove it, she thought, remembering the day she'd run in to him. At the time she'd found it funny. Now the joke was on her.

Before either of her friends could respond, her phone rang again.

"Oh, my God," Sam said. "You need to turn this thing off." Sam read the call display again. "This one's from Brenda Billings. Isn't she your...?"

"My Realtor." Claire grabbed the phone. "I do have to take this call. We put an offer on the house this morning—"

She jumped up and crossed the room to the sliding doors that overlooked Kristi's patio. "Brenda, hi. Thanks for calling. Any news?"

"Yes, I have, and it's good news. They accepted your offer, including all the conditions. They're moving out of the city at the end of the month, so they've even agreed to the early possession date you asked for."

"Oh, um, wow. That's good. Really good." A few hours ago she had wanted this so much it hurt. Now she wanted to feel happy about it, and couldn't. It was all too much. Being with Luke, the maybe baby and now a new home.

"Claire? Is everything okay?"

She whipped off her glasses and dabbed the corners of her eyes with her sleeve. "Fine. Everything's fine. I'm right in the middle of something, though. Can we meet, tomorrow maybe, to go over the details?"

"Of course we can. How's ten? Or is that too early?"

"No, that'll be perfect."

"Would you like me to come to your place?"

"Um, no. I have to run errands first thing. Can we meet at my office instead?" Since Brenda hadn't asked, Claire assumed she hadn't seen the evening news, and she didn't know if she could get back into her building tomorrow morning.

"Your office tomorrow at ten. See you then. And Claire…?"

"Mmm-hmm?"

"Congratulations! You just bought a house."

"Thanks."

She turned back to Kristi and Sam, who looked as though they were waiting to pounce.

"I got the house."

Then they were on their feet, she was sandwiched in a group hug, and they took turns assuring her that she was doing the right thing.

"So happy for you."

"It's a perfect house for you."

"A chance for a fresh new start."

"We're going to throw the most awesome housewarming party."

A housewarming party. That would be fun. But not as much fun as a baby shower. With that thought, she gave in to the tears, although she couldn't have said if they were happy or sad.

THE SKY WAS TURNING from dusk to dark when Luke left Claire's condo. The patrol cars, barricades and crime scene tape were gone and the street was quiet as he led Rex out the front door and onto the sidewalk. Everything back to normal. And then the hair on his neck went up.

Donald? Had to be, he decided, making a show of looking around as he hitched his duffel bag onto his shoulder and unclipped Rex's lead. *Bring it on, asshole.*

He spotted the Lexus halfway down the block. In this light the driver's side appeared empty, but he couldn't be sure. He'd parked his truck on the next block so he had to walk past Donald's car anyway. Not that he needed an excuse, and the mood he was in right now, it would be best for Claire's ex if he was inside the car. With the doors locked.

His first instinct was right. The car was unoccupied, but Donald was there. He stepped out of a recessed doorway as Luke approached.

Luke stopped walking. "Rex, watch." The dog immediately halted and fixed his sights on Donald. "Good dog."

"Nice night to walk your dog."

"What do you want, Robinson?"

"I want to know what the hell went on here this afternoon. Claire isn't answering her phone and I wanted to make sure she's okay."

"Claire's fine." Although he doubted that was any more true for her than it was for him.

"What about the police raid?"

"What about it?" He was in no mood for questions, even less so for small talk. "If you saw the news, then you know what went down. Nothing more I can tell you."

"Bull." Donald shifted, giving the appearance that he was stepping forward.

Rex flattened his ears and growled.

Donald took a step back instead. "What's with your dog?"

"I don't think he likes you."

"He should be on a leash."

And you should be in a jail cell. "Rex won't move… unless I tell him to."

Donald fished his keys out of his jacket pocket. "I have to get going."

"Good plan."

"If you see Claire, tell her—" Whatever the message, he seemed to decide against having Luke relay it.

"I'll tell her I ran into you."

Donald got into his car and made a show of peeling away from the curb. The jerk.

"Good boy." Rex followed him to the truck, hopped in when Luke opened the passenger door for him.

Luke tossed his duffel bag in the back and then, behind the wheel, it was all he could do to resist squealing his own tires as he slammed the truck into gear and drove away from what was, without a doubt, the best thing that had ever happened to him.

Twenty minutes later, after he'd dropped Rex and the rest of his stuff at his place and swapped the truck for the Ducati, he stood on the sidewalk in front of a downtown liquor store.

In the two years since he'd quit drinking, this was hands down the stupidest thing he'd ever done. Hell, he hadn't even done anything yet, but he was on the precipice of a long, slippery slope.

Let yourself slide and you might never make it back up.

You don't know that, not for sure. Maybe one night, one slip off the wagon wouldn't be so bad.

Listen to yourself. Is this what you want?

No. He wanted Claire. But right now he wanted this more. He wanted to wallow in self-pity and guilt awhile, until the booze let him talk himself into believing that none of this was his fault, and then finally have it wrap its silky tentacles around his consciousness until he no longer felt anything.

He pulled out his phone to see if he'd missed a call from Claire. He hadn't. Then he scrolled through the numbers in his contact list, paused at hers before he kept going, not even sure what he was looking for until he found it.

Norman G. His AA sponsor.

We admitted we were powerless over alcohol—that our lives had become unmanageable.

After two years, after all the work he'd done, how the hell had he ended up back at step one? He hit the call button, listened as Norm's phone rang, felt his heart do a dip in his chest when it went to voice mail.

"Norm. It's Luke D. I'm…"

What? What could he say? *I'm this close to throwing the past two years down the toilet?*

"I'm taking it one day at a time. Some shit went down today, but I'm okay. I'm not going to hit the bottle." He'd hit the road instead.

Helmet on, he revved the Ducati, roared away from the curb and headed for the exit to the I-5. Where to go? North? Canada, maybe? South to Oregon? The lack of a passport in his pocket made it an easy decision. After he eased the Ducati onto the freeway, he opened her up and gave himself up to the ride. It was the only other way he knew to get numb.

CLAIRE WOKE IN KRISTI'S daughter's room, vacant because Jenna had been at a sleepover. The rest of the house, judging by the commotion, was wide-awake. Water running, footsteps racing down the hallway, dogs barking and Kristi shushing everyone.

Grateful as she was that she hadn't had to go home last night to an empty apartment and the risk of running into Luke, she now needed to be alone. Quietly she slipped out of bed and into the bathroom down the hall, which was mercifully free. After a quick shower she put on the clothes she'd worn yesterday, brushed her hair and dabbed on some lip gloss, which was the only thing she could find in her handbag.

Kristi was coming down the hallway with a cup of coffee when she emerged from the bathroom. "Good morning. How'd you sleep?"

"Not bad." Better than she'd expected.

"I thought you might like some coffee. It's decaf." Kristi winked. "Just in case."

"Thanks, but you didn't have to. I should go."

"I know. I assumed you'd want to avoid the Callahan-McTavish household's Saturday-morning madness, and I thought you might like to have something while you get ready but it looks like you already are."

"I hope you don't mind."

"Of course not! You have a busy day ahead, what with buying a new house and all. A good thing, given everything that's happened." Kristi set the coffee cup on a hall table and hugged her. "Have you listened to Luke's message yet?"

"No." She'd been tempted to last night after she'd crawled into bed, but was afraid to trust her reaction to hearing his voice. She had avoided it again this morning for the same reason. "I'll wait until I'm home."

"I completely understand. Will you call me after you've sealed the deal on the house?"

"I will." In spite of her momentary panic last night, she knew it was the right thing to do. The house was exactly what she'd dreamed of, practically perfect, really, and the few things that weren't quite right could easily be made so, especially with Sam and Kristi's help.

"And you'll call after you listen to Luke's message?"

That actually made Claire laugh. "You really want a report on that?"

"Sweetie, I'm thrilled about the house, you know that, but I'm dying to hear what Luke has to say. And you need to give him a chance to explain, especially under these circumstances." She gave Claire's belly a playful pat.

"Okay, okay, I'll call. Just don't hold your breath."

"Come on, I'll walk you out to your car."

You really do have the best friends in the world, Claire told herself as she backed out of Kristi's driveway. She was leaving a lot of things behind, mostly unpleasant ones, and heading into a future filled with equal parts excitement and uncertainty. Knowing her friends wouldn't let her go it alone made all the difference.

LUKE WOKE THAT MORNING with a clear head, a heavy conscience and a dog who was ready for a run.

"First things first." He pulled on the jeans and T-shirt he'd stripped off and tossed on the floor a few hours ago, brushed his teeth and went into the kitchen.

He pulled open the fridge, snagged the milk carton and opened the spout. He checked the expiration date before he took a swig and poured the contents down the sink. Good thing he took his coffee black, he thought as he filled a pot with water, turned on the stove and snagged a jar of instant out of the cupboard. Just a week, and he'd already become accustomed to all the fancy gadgets in Claire's kitchen.

Mostly, though, he missed her. Missed waking up to the warm body next to his, the mind-blowing morning sex, the cozying up for coffee afterward. He'd screwed up, and other than apologizing he didn't know how to fix it. Maybe he couldn't. Or maybe he shouldn't even try.

He spooned coffee crystals into a mug while he waited for the water to boil. He'd been close to having a drink last night. Somehow he'd found enough inner strength to talk himself out of it, but next time he might not be so lucky. And there would always be a next time. What if he couldn't stop himself?

One day at a time, they said. At least he'd figured it out last night. But then he'd hit the highway and lost himself in the adrenaline rush of high speed on the open road. That had been stupid, and completely irresponsible.

Claire didn't deserve that. He didn't deserve her. He needed to apologize to her, even try to explain why he'd let his team believe he had "sweet-talked" her into letting him stay with her, and why, for the sake of the investigation but also for her own safety, he hadn't been able to tell her what and who they had under surveillance.

Be willing to make amends. Huh. Back to step eight already. More like back to step eight *again*.

He found his phone in his jacket pocket, checked it for messages. A voice mail from Wong saying there was a meeting at one o'clock. Another from his sponsor, offering to meet for coffee that morning. And a text from Cam, apologizing for the screwup. Nothing from Claire. No surprise there.

How was he supposed to handle this? He had more experience with effing things up than fixing them. He had already left her a message. Now he needed a Plan B because if he kept calling, he'd be as bad as Donald. She didn't need any more of that kind of crap in her life.

Send her flowers? Right, because this was just like a birthday.

He still had the key to her condo—he'd needed to lock the dead bolt on the way out. Would she let him give it back in person? That might be his best, and only, shot. Now to figure out the timing. Best to give her twenty-four hours to respond to the message he'd left yesterday. Then, if he didn't hear from her, he would send her a text message about the key, and he'd make a point of letting her know he had no intention of using it.

Rex jabbed Luke's leg with his snout. "I know, buddy. We both need to let off some steam."

He'd change into sweats, pound the pavement for half an

hour. Then he'd grab coffee and get a pep talk from Norman, go to his meeting. After that, if he still hadn't heard from Claire, he'd move on to Plan B.

Chapter Twelve

Two weeks after sealing the deal on her new home, Claire stood in the middle of her kitchen and surveyed the stacks of cardboard boxes, all neatly taped shut and labelled with their contents. The movers would be here in the morning and tonight would be her last night in the penthouse condo that had never quite felt like home.

Chloe sat hunched on a stool, eyeing the piles with disdain.

"You're going to love our new home." Claire stroked the soft fur on the top of her head. "I know you don't believe that now, but you'll see. The dining room has a big window with a window seat that looks out onto the back garden, and you can sit there and watch the birds."

She had always wanted a window seat, and it was just one of the many things about the house that made it so right for her. By some miracle—and she didn't even believe in miracles but she couldn't think of a better way to describe it—Brenda Billings, her Realtor, had found a buyer for the condo, despite its hefty price tag and the fact that a mere two weeks ago the police had raided a brothel in the next building. She still had difficulty wrapping her head around that one. The owners weren't taking possession for two months, but Donald had agreed to the sale in spite of his now obvious financial woes.

The divorce papers had been signed, and although the Beatrix Potter book had stayed in Claire's possession, Donald still called or sent a text message about it every day, sometimes both and often more than once. She deleted them as they came in and did her best to ignore them, and would have found it laughable that a grown man was fixated on a children's book if he wasn't so darned annoying.

AFTER SHE'D FINALIZED the purchase on the house, she had listened to Luke's first phone message. He had apologized, offered an explanation about wanting to protect her, which was why he hadn't told her about doing surveillance and hadn't told his colleagues about their relationship. A truckload of manure as far as she was concerned. She had already known he was working undercover, and what possible difference could their relationship make to a handful of other police officers? The truth was obvious. He hadn't mentioned the surveillance to her in case she said no, and he hadn't mentioned the relationship to his colleagues because there was no relationship. He'd only let her believe it was about the two of them. And about making sure Donald left her alone, so make that two truckloads.

The day after Luke left that message, he had texted her with an offer to come by or meet her someplace to return the key. She had sidestepped that by telling him to drop it off at the Ready Set Sold office. He had done as she'd asked and she had made a point of not being there, although she'd been given an earful by their office manager. Marlie had called her the instant he'd left, gushing about what a "gorgeous hunk of manhood" he was and admonishing Claire for letting him get away.

But Claire hadn't let him go, she'd sent him packing, and it had been the right thing to do. Somewhat to her surprise, he hadn't given up. Every day he'd sent a text message, always in the evening after she'd finished doing some packing and was getting settled for the night. At first they were short and to the point.

Left the key with your secretary.

The next day he'd written, *I get that you don't want to see me. If you change your mind, can I buy you a latte?*

After she ignored those, the messages became less serious.

Rex would like to know if Chloe misses him.

Rex wants to know if there are any dog biscuits left.

Since he hasn't heard from Chloe, Rex wonders if he's in the doghouse, too.

His pattern had become predictable, and she found herself looking forward to the message. It was schoolgirl silly, but it was true.

Sam and Kristi insisted the messages meant he was genuinely sorry for what he'd done, that he wanted a second chance, and that Claire should give him one. But she couldn't let herself do that. Not yet.

She still needed to take a pregnancy test, but she had decided to wait until she was in her new home. If she was having Luke's baby, and in her heart she hoped she was, then she wanted that news to be connected to her new home, not the condo. She had too many negative associations with this place. The house represented a fresh start, a new chapter in her life. If that included the baby she had dreamed about for so long, she was ready for it. And fully prepared to raise a child on her own, since she knew Luke didn't want to be part of a fresh start with her.

And that's why she couldn't reply to his messages. Not until she knew for sure, one way or the other. It had been three weeks since the first night they'd slept together, she still hadn't had a period, and she'd felt queasy when she got up that morning. Those things could be due to stress, or they could mean she was having a baby.

The pregnancy test she'd bought that morning had been tucked away in her handbag, and tomorrow the waiting would be over. After that she would have to answer one of the two big questions.

If she wasn't pregnant, should she respond to Luke's messages? Consider letting him back into her life? The part of her that had recklessly become *that woman* a couple of weeks ago screamed *yes!* But her sensible side reminded her there was no future with a man who couldn't commit to a family.

If she was expecting, then she needed to figure out how to tell Luke, and when. Claire was inclined to wait, but Sam was emphatic that he needed to know right away. She had made a similar mistake, not telling her husband, AJ, about their son, Will, and they had lost three precious years of being together as a family.

There was no danger of Luke wanting a family, he had already made it perfectly clear he didn't, but of course he had a right to know. And Claire always did the right thing. She just needed to work on the timing.

"La Cucaracha" blaring on her phone dragged her back to the present. This time it was a text message.

Doesn't make sense to have so much money tied up in an old book. Willing to split the $$ when we sell it. Call me.

"Oh. My. God." She deleted the message, wishing she hadn't read it at all. "We're not discussing this, ever, and *we* are not divvying up any money because *I* am not selling the book." What part of this did he not understand?

The book was still locked in the safe at the office, and she had already decided to keep it there until Donald got his share from the sale of the condo. He and Deirdre were obviously having financial problems, but Claire hoped he would forget about the book once he received his share from the sale of the condo.

She ran a hand over her belly. "Maybe I'll have someone to read it to." Maybe.

A month ago she would never have believed she could be hoping and praying to be pregnant. Now the prospect of raising a child on her own held none of the worry it would have then, and she knew why. She couldn't have the man she loved, but if she could have his baby, she would love their child with all her heart.

If there was a baby.

She scooped Chloe into her arms and held her close in spite of the animal's loud and vigorous protest. "Please let there be a baby," she whispered. "Please."

LUKE SLOWED THE TRUCK to a crawl and scanned both sides of the street as he drove past Claire's condominium complex. No sign of the Lexus. Either Donald had backed off, or he was being more discreet now that he knew Luke was onto him.

Every day since Claire had told him to get out, Luke had driven by, sometimes more than once. He hated that he did it, but he wasn't looking for Claire. Or so he kept telling himself. He was keeping an eye on Donald.

He had also sent her a text message every day, and although she had only responded to the first one, with instructions for returning her key, he was sure she read them. He wanted to do more, but aside from making sure Donald wasn't hanging around, there wasn't much else he could do.

He already knew what he'd say in tonight's text message, though.

Should he send her a housewarming gift, too? Or would that be too much?

Probably too much. He wouldn't know what to give her, anyway.

Another children's book? She had so many already, he wouldn't have a clue where to start. Still not a bad idea, though. He'd file that one away for future reference.

This would be the last time he needed to come here. The day he'd dropped off her key, he had found out from the woman who worked in her office that she had purchased the house she'd been so excited about and would be moving at the end of the month. The woman, who had introduced herself as Marlie, probably would have spilled more information if he had asked. But she also would have told her boss, he had no doubt of that. She had referred to Claire as one of her angels—she called the three women Marlie's angels—which suggested they had a close bond and a good working relationship. He wouldn't expect anything less of Claire.

The only thing he couldn't figure out was how she'd ended up with a jerk like Donald Robinson. She was beautiful, smart and sexy as hell, and she was a good person. Hardworking, honest—not exactly the first things to come to mind with a real estate agent, but no doubt it was those qualities that made her so successful at it.

It killed him to think she'd been date-raped back in college, but he hated the idea of her being with Donald almost as much. That sick son of a bitch's hands on that knockout body was pure torture, the long drawn-out kind that started as a slow burn deep in his gut. The hotter it got, the further it spread, until it cut off his breath. Like it was doing right now.

Claire believed that selling the condo and moving into a place of her own would put an end to any further communication from Donald. Luke doubted it would, but for her sake he hoped she was right.

Luke cruised past her building and sure enough, there was a moving van parked in front, back doors open, and a man was pushing a dolly loaded with boxes up the ramp.

Did Donald know she was moving today? Most likely, but the better question was did he know where she was moving? When she'd shown Luke the real estate listing, he had made a mental note of the address and had already scoped out the neighborhood. Unlike the busy streets downtown, if Donald hung around Claire's new place in that fancy car of his, he'd stick out like a snowman in July. Did the guy have enough smarts to realize that? Hard to say, but in case he didn't, Luke intended to keep an eye on him.

THE MOVE WENT OFF WITHOUT a hitch. For the past two weeks, Claire had spent practically every waking moment organizing and packing. It had paid off today, and it had also helped her keep her mind off Luke. Having the support of the two best friends in the world was also a help. Make that a godsend.

"Have I told you how much I love this house?" Kristi was unpacking table linens into the bottom drawer of the vintage sideboard Claire had found online.

Claire unwrapped the silverware chest Nonna DeAngelo had given her and set it on top of the sideboard. "Once or twice."

"Or ten," Sam added.

Kristi made a face at her.

Sam responded with one of her own. "Hey, I love it, too. I just don't wear my heart on my sleeve."

They made Claire laugh, and she loved them for it. They had been waiting here when the moving van pulled up, had already helped her unpack and organize the kitchen. They intended to stay until Claire took the pregnancy test, and she wouldn't have it any other way.

Sam finished replacing the switch plate cover, stuck her screwdriver in her back pocket and tested the dimmer switch she'd just installed.

"It works," Claire said.

"Of course it works."

"That's such a pretty chandelier," Kristi said, closing the drawer. "And that's the last box we had to unpack in here."

"Good. It's time we took a break." Claire went into the kitchen and returned with three chilled bottles of water and a vegetable tray and dip she'd picked up at the deli. "Let's sit," she said, setting them on the dining room table.

Sam unscrewed the top of her bottle and took a long drink as she settled onto one of the chairs. "Ah. I needed that."

"Me, too." Kristi joined her. "Mmm, nice and cold. Sit," she said to Claire, patting the chair next to her.

She could use a break but she was antsy and on edge, partly energized by the exciting newness of all this, but mostly anxious about the pregnancy test. She was all but convinced she was pregnant, and she would be disappointed—no, devastated—if she wasn't.

She took the chair next to Kristi, though, and sipped some water.

"This might be a good time to show you the plans I've been working on for your attic." Sam dipped a celery stick and crunched. "You might not want to do the work right away, but it's something to consider."

"Let's see what you've got." She and Kristi leaned in to look at Sam's drawings.

"The access hatch to the attic is in the hallway so that's a perfect place to put in the pull-down stairs. There's enough clearance to install a ceiling down the center of the attic, under the peak of the roof, then follow the slope down to sidewalls that would be about four feet high."

"My kids would love a space like that," Kristi said. "It would make a great playroom."

The idea of a child's playroom caught Claire's imagination, too. And triggered a memory. "You know, it reminds me of a house we rented near one of the air force bases where my dad was stationed. I'm not sure where, we moved so many times, but I remember my sister and I loved the pull-down staircase. My mom helped me and my sister set it up as our own little hideaway, complete with bean bag chairs and Bon Jovi and Madonna posters. It's been years since I've thought about that."

"Wow, you had a cool mom." Sam, who'd been raised by a mother who struggled with mental illness, looked a little wistful. She slid the drawings off her clipboard and gave them to Claire. "I wrote up a supply list and cost estimate, too. You have plenty of room in this house, but you can think about it for the future. And opening up more space always adds value."

"I'll definitely think about it for down the road. And it's not like you'll be able to do any major construction right now, not until after the baby is born."

Sam laughed and shook her head. "Now you sound like AJ. He'd have me on bed rest, if he could, but my doctor says I'm in great shape. I'm still running, just not as hard and not as far as I used to, and I should be able to keep working right up until the baby's born."

"That may be the case, but I still think you should think about hiring an assistant," Claire said. "At least a helper who can do all the heavy lifting for you."

Kristi munched on a carrot. "I totally agree."

"I've been thinking the same thing," Sam said. "And

I'd like both of you to be in on the interviews when I do. And whoever we hire will have to have a good range of skills, not just be 'helper.' I'll want to take some time off after the baby's born, so the person we hire will have to be a good fit for all of us."

"That's a really good idea." Claire swiped a broccoli floret through the dip, popped it into her mouth and wiped her fingers on a paper napkin. She hadn't eaten since breakfast, hadn't even thought of food, which was unlike her, and she hadn't realized how hungry she was.

"Speaking of babies," Kristi said. "You do know Sam and I aren't leaving until you put us out of our misery and take that pregnancy test."

Claire knew exactly how they felt. "I know, and I'm not sure why I keep putting it off. I guess I want everything here to be done and perfect, so when I find out that I am...*if* I'm pregnant, then I won't have to think about anything else."

"You really are hoping it's positive, aren't you?"

"I am. Is that crazy? Am I crazy?"

"No!"

"Definitely not."

"I've always had this romantic vision of me living in a house with a white picket fence and having a cat and a dog and a family."

"You're halfway there," Sam said.

"At one time I believed I'd have all those things with Donald." She caught her friends exchanging a look. "I know, what was I thinking? So I gave up on the dream, but then Luke came along and..."

"And you really do love him, don't you?" Kristi asked.

She fought the lump forming in her throat. "I do."

"Are you still getting text messages from him?"

Claire smiled. She couldn't help herself. "I am."

"Have you replied to any of them?"

"Not yet. I mean, what's the point? If I'm pregnant, he will freak out. And if I'm not—"

"You'll freak out," Kristi said.

"Funny. I was going to say that if I'm not, do I want to be involved with someone who isn't interested in having a relationship?"

Sam grinned. "When that someone looks like he does? Um…yeah, you do."

"All these what-ifs are making me crazy." Kristi snagged another carrot and stood up. "If this place has to be perfect before we can find out if you're having a baby, then we need to get back to work. What's next?" she asked.

Claire reached for her iPad and brought up her check-list. "The kitchen, dining room and my bedroom are done. Everything's in place in the living room, I just need to figure out where I want to hang pictures. And the boxes of stuff for the bathroom and linen closet still need to be unpacked."

Kristi picked up her water bottle. "I'll look after the bathroom while the two of you finish up in the living room."

"Good plan." Sam got up and reached for her toolbox.

"And when we're finished, I'll order pizza for dinner."

Sam grabbed her by the arm and steered her into the living room. "No way. When we're finished, we'll find out if you're having a baby. *Then* you can order pizza."

Chapter Thirteen

"Please tell me we're done," Sam said an hour later. "Everything's unpacked, Kristi flattened all the boxes and put them in the garage, I even fixed that loose floorboard on the veranda. If you find another excuse to keep us in suspense, you might as well just shoot me."

"There's just one more thing," Kristi said. "Sorry, Sam! I'm anxious, too, but we forgot about Claire's housewarming present. It's out in my van."

"Right." Sam carried her toolbox outside. "I'll put this away in my truck while you get the gift."

"You've both done so much already, a gift isn't necessary," Claire said.

Kristi dug her camera out of her bag and looped the strap around her neck. "Come on," she said, taking Claire's arm. "We need you outside, too."

Curious, Claire stood on the veranda and waited until her friends returned with a large, flat package wrapped in brown paper and tied up with raffia.

"Sam and I worked on it together, so it's one of a kind."

Claire slipped off the wrapping and managed to catch a glimpse of a wreath for her front door before her tears blurred her eyes. Happy tears. She took off her glasses, wiped her eyes, took a closer look at the gift.

"It's beautiful, and it's exactly right." It was made of

wood, with a miniature cutout of the actual house in the center, painted yellow with a red door, a white picket fence in front and *Home Sweet Home* spelled out in painted wooden letters around the outside.

"Oh, you guys. Thank you. I love it." She hugged them both at the same time. "Everything really is perfect now." She had left the wreath on the door at the condo, deciding this house deserved something a little more special. And now it had it.

Sam took the wreath from her and hung it on the door, on a hook she must have installed while she was out here nailing down floorboards.

Kristi folded the paper wrapping and took the lens cap off her camera, and Sam joined her on the sidewalk in front of the house. "Picture time. I want to take one of you on the veranda, right there by the front door, next to the wreath."

"I'm a mess!" Claire said. She was wearing old jeans and a baggy sweatshirt and hadn't combed her hair in hours.

"You're not, you look gorgeous, and this is not a portrait. This is one of those special moments that needs to be recorded."

Knowing Kristi was right, that this was a photograph she would cherish forever, she went along with them. And then she joined her friends on the sidewalk, gazed back at the house with the newly adorned red door and started to cry all over again.

"All these tears," Sam said, linking arms with her. "You must be pregnant."

Kristi took her other arm. "Let's find out."

They went inside and led her down the hall to the bathroom.

"In you go," Sam said. "We'll be right outside the door."

Kristi gave her a gentle shove through the doorway. "I put the box on the counter."

Sam tapped her wrist. "Let us know as soon as you've, you know, done your thing, and I'll set my stopwatch."

"This might not work," Claire said, feeling she needed to warn them, and caution herself. "It says it's best to do it first thing in the morning."

"Enough with the excuses already." Sam laughed. "You're killing me here."

"If it's negative, we'll come back in the morning and do another one," Kristi said, pulling the door closed.

Feeling light-headed and a little giddy, Claire opened the package. She had already read the instructions at least a dozen times, so she "did her thing" and opened the door.

Sam set her watch.

"The instructions say it takes—"

"Oh, I know how long it takes. Did one of these myself a couple of months ago."

Kristi took the stick from Claire and held it behind her back. "Was AJ in on it, too?"

"Of course. We didn't get to do any of these things together when I was expecting Will. This time he doesn't want to miss a thing."

Not Luke, Claire thought. He hadn't taken their relationship seriously in the first place, and he didn't want kids at all. Would there be a time when he regretted not being part of this baby's beginning, if there was a baby? She would always regret that he wasn't here.

Kristi sighed. "I still think you and AJ, reconnecting after all that time, finding out he's the one who adopted Will…it's like a modern-day fairy tale."

Sam rolled her eyes. "Or a soap opera."

"No way. When have you ever seen a happily-ever-after in one of the soaps? Yours is definitely a fairy tale."

Sam's stopwatch beeped.

"Ready?" Kristi asked.

More than ready. "I've been ready forever."

Sam took one hand and squeezed.

Please, please, please...

Kristi took her other hand, pulled the stick around so she could read it. Her eyes filled with tears. "Girl, you're having a baby."

One of them screamed, or maybe all of them did, and then Claire found herself in the most exuberant group hug ever. Together they laughed and cried and jumped up and down.

Sam gushed about how much fun they would have shopping for baby clothes, planning their nurseries, comparing baby bumps.

Kristi insisted that, even though she wasn't pregnant... yet...she be included, and especially that she be consulted on designing their nurseries. "This is going to be so much fun!"

Finally they made their way to the kitchen, and Claire realized she was starving. "I really need to have something to eat, and I did promise you pizza."

"Pizza? To celebrate this kind of news? No way," Sam said. "We need to go out and do this up right."

"I agree," Kristi said, ponytail bobbing. "Someplace fancy because we have two babies to celebrate."

Claire couldn't say why exactly but she was reluctant to go out. Maybe it was the newness of her new home, or maybe it was the baby news. One she wasn't ready to leave, and the other she wasn't ready to share with the world.

"Look at us," she said. "Grungy work clothes, not to

mention my hair's a mess and I'm not wearing any makeup." She hadn't put any on that morning because she had suspected it would be an emotional day, filled with happy tears, and she had been right.

"True," Kristi said, looking down at her cropped yoga pants and bright yellow sneakers. "And it would take forever for me and Sam to go home, shower and change, and get back here."

"You're right. Pizza it is, but we need to plan a special night out, sometime this week."

Relieved that her friends weren't disappointed, Claire hunted down her phone and did a search for pizza places in the neighborhood.

"They'll be here in twenty minutes." She set her phone down and gripped the edge of the kitchen counter, suddenly feeling faint.

"Whoa, you're looking a little shaky." Sam grabbed her shoulders and held on. "How much have you had to eat today?"

"Not much, I'm afraid."

Kristi slipped an arm around her waist. "Come on. We'll go sit in the living room, get you comfy and wait for the pizza. And no more dieting," she added. "You're eating for two now."

Dieting had been the last thing on her mind today. She usually thought about food way more often than she should, but today she'd been too busy, too excited. And now she was even more light-headed than she'd felt in the bathroom, and something in her stomach was doing cartwheels.

Sam turned on the gas fireplace and Kristi got her settled in the armchair next to it. Aside from the little break they'd taken earlier, she hadn't sat down all day. Kristi was right. She really would have to take better care of herself.

Her friends brought in plates, napkins and bottled water from the kitchen, and after the pizzas arrived they flipped open the boxes and dug in. Silence reigned for several minutes and then, somewhat satisfied after the first few bites, they chatted and laughed and shared pregnancy and baby stories. Claire soaked up the warmth of her new living room with its beautiful bay window and brick fireplace with a wide mantel. Then she turned her attention to her two best friends, laughed at their baby stories and decided she had to be the luckiest woman in world. She might not have the man she loved, but she had a lot…a lot more than most…and she was surrounded by people she loved and who loved her.

"Either I was really, really hungry or that was the best pizza I've ever tasted." Sam crumpled her napkin into a ball and tossed it into an empty box.

"I think it was both." Kristi flopped back on the sofa and patted her stomach. "I'm stuffed now, though. And we should probably get going and let you get some rest. But before we go, we have one more present for you."

"Another one?" After the wreath they'd given her, she couldn't imagine a single thing she needed.

"This one's not for the house, though. It's for you." Kristi pulled a gift bag out of the enormous tote bag she always carried around with her. "We didn't give it to you sooner because this is for you and the baby."

Inside the bag were two books, one filled with baby names, another that claimed to contain everything a woman needed to know about pregnancy. Once again Claire's eyes filled with tears, and she decided this had to be hormonal because she'd been weepier today than she'd been in years. She got to her feet and there was more hugging and even more tears as she thanked them. Then they cleared away the pizza boxes and she walked with them to the door.

After Sam and Kristi left, she locked the front door. It was silly to still be worried about Donald. He hadn't come back to the condo, at least not as far as she knew, and since she'd changed the locks, he couldn't get in anyway. He might keep calling but he wouldn't come here. Would he? No. To her knowledge, he didn't know where she'd moved. Luke had been worried about him, but then his motives weren't so pure, either.

Just to reassure herself, she went through the kitchen and made sure the back door was locked, too. Then she returned to the living room and settled back into the armchair by the fireplace and swung her feet onto the ottoman. Chloe, who'd been hiding under the bed since they'd arrived in the morning, stalked into the room and gave a cautious look around. Apparently now that the house was quiet, she was feeling braver, or at least less freaked out by all the changes.

Claire patted her lap and the cat jumped up to join her. "Good girl," she said, enjoying the company.

For a few moments she simply gazed at the fire. As happy as she was, today held a bittersweetness that wouldn't to go away anytime soon. Luke had never been hers to lose, but not having him in her life left a hole that was never likely to be filled. Still, there was much to be grateful for, she thought, as once again she took in her new surroundings. She had this cozy new home, she had friends who would always be here for her and best of all she was having a baby.

"Don't get too set in your ways too soon," she whispered to the cat. "The changes haven't stopped yet."

On the side table next to her chair, her phone vibrated. She picked it up and read the message.

Home sweet home?

Yes, Luke. Home sweet home.

LUKE HIT THE SEND BUTTON on his phone, tossed it onto a pile of newspapers on the coffee table and picked up the TV remote. No sense waiting for Claire to reply. He knew she wouldn't.

Was it a mistake to let her know that he knew she had moved today? He hoped not. Besides, her secretary would have told her about their conversation, he was sure of that. He'd like to know what she thought of the messages he'd been sending every day. Did she read them? He was pretty sure she did. He was kind of disappointed she didn't reply, but on the bright side she hadn't told him to get lost.

He surfed through a dozen channels while he debated whether to stay in or go out. Better stay home. If he went out this late, he would either drive past Claire's new place or he would drive by a liquor store, and he had no business doing either. Staying sober these past couple of weeks had been harder than any other time in the past two years.

At least work had kept him busy. Phong remained in custody, bail denied. The team had wrapped up the interview with Phong's girls, mostly with the help of translators, and written up their statements. Then there was all the forensic work on the apartment itself, which was still a crime scene, and the inventory of all the drugs and cash that had been confiscated. Most of the reports should be wrapped in the coming week, and then he'd have a little more free time.

He and the team had worked toward this bust for months

and he hated that he wasn't more stoked about the outcome, and he only had himself to blame. He couldn't seem to move past this screwup with Claire, and he didn't know why. He should probably stop communicating with her. He sent a message at the same time every evening, when he knew she was winding down after a long, busy day, likely getting ready to go to bed. If she said she didn't miss him, he'd believe her. Their rhythms had been in perfect sync, though, and if she said she didn't miss the intimacy, she'd be lying. Until he found a way to pick up where they left off, he figured that reminding her of those shared intimacies right before she went to bed was his best shot at keeping himself on her radar.

He got up off the couch, laughing at Rex, who stretched his hind legs over the spot he'd just vacated. After one last futile check for messages, he headed for the bedroom.

"'Night, Rex. Maybe we'll hear from her tomorrow."

The dog's one-eyed examination suggested he didn't believe it any more than Luke did. It really was time to come up with a better plan.

THREE DAYS AFTER SHE'D moved into her new house, Claire was stuck in traffic on her way home from the office. The route she'd tried yesterday had been slow. Today she was at a standstill. She had plenty of time, though, and this gave her a chance to think about what to wear tonight because, true to their word, Sam and Kristi made a reservation at one of their favorite downtown restaurants.

"We're going totally glam," Kristi had insisted. "While you and Sam can still fit into your glamorous clothes."

Claire smiled at that, trying to think of the last time she'd seen Sam in anything other than jeans and a work shirt. Probably not since her wedding, which had been a small, intimate affair with only family and a handful of friends. Sam had worn a sleeveless, cream-colored satin shift, knee-length, with matching pumps and the stunning ruby pendant earrings that had been AJ's wedding gift to his beautiful bride. It turned out that Sam, understated and elegant that day, had been hiding a knockout figure under those work duds of hers, and the groom hadn't been able to take his eyes off her.

Claire accelerated slowly as traffic started to move again.

Of the three of them, Kristi was, without question, the girliest. Knowing her, she'd probably sat down at her sewing machine last night and whipped up something brand-new, one-of-a-kind and totally eye-popping.

Claire still had no idea what she would wear tonight. She had several basic black dresses in her wardrobe and each of them had been a very safe choice. Black was classic, it worked for any occasion, and it was slimming. In theory, at least. Ever since that week with Luke, she'd been wishing she had something sexier in her closet. She had actually splurged on some new lingerie but that had been the day of the raid on her condominium complex, and she hadn't had a chance to test-drive it.

She would dig it out and wear it tonight. There was no law that said a girl couldn't feel good about herself, even though she was just having dinner with friends. She was still pondering what to wear over the lingerie as she turned onto her street. The sight of two police cruisers parked halfway down the block had her braking and flashing back to a couple of weeks ago when she'd come home to find the condominium complex surrounded by police vehicles.

Déjà vu I can live with, but please don't let this have anything to do with my house. Or, God forbid, Luke.

Her dread increased, though, as she drove slowly down the street. The police cars with their lights flashing were parked right in front of her place and a police officer stood in her front yard, talking on a radio. Several neighbors she hadn't even met yet were clustered across the street.

Great introduction to the neighborhood, she thought as she pulled up and jumped out of her car. "Is there a problem here?" she asked, walking through the open gate.

"Ma'am." The guy tipped his hat. "Is this your home?"

"Yes, it is. I just moved in on the weekend."

"I'm afraid to tell you that you've had an intruder. One of your neighbors called it in."

Someone was in her house? Her first thought was for Chloe. "My cat—" She started for the front door.

The officer stepped in front of her. "Sorry, ma'am. I have to ask you to wait here until the house is clear. Two officers are inside right now."

"Inside? How?"

"Seems the intruder climbed in through an unsecured window."

An unsecured window? She was pretty sure she hadn't even opened any of the windows, it wasn't warm enough. But had she checked to make sure they were locked? No, she was sure she hadn't. What was she thinking? Someone could have broken in while she was there, sleeping even. To wake up and know someone was in her home… her skin crawled.

A voice crackled from the officer's radio, but Claire couldn't make out what was being said.

"The intruder has been apprehended," he said. "They're bringing him out now. Would you rather wait in your car, ma'am? They'll be taking him down to the station, and then we can go inside with you, make sure everything's as it should be."

It had to be a random break-and-enter, so did she want

the intruder to see her? No, not at all, so waiting in the car was probably a good idea.

She had her hand on the door handle when two more officers appeared from the side of the house, escorting a man…

Was that…

"Donald?" Not thinking clearly and not caring one little bit, she rushed toward them. The officers had Donald by both arms and… Ha! His hands were cuffed behind his back, and for once he actually looked cowed.

"You broke into my house?" Anger and disgust bubbled up inside her. "How do you even know where I live? Have you been following me?"

The officer who'd been standing on the lawn quickly stepped up and took her arm, preventing her from getting any closer. "You know this man?"

"Unfortunately, I do. He's my ex-husband." At least that part was fortunate. "Emphasis on *ex*," she said, watching them secure the loser in the backseat of one of the cruisers. One officer got behind the wheel, the other, a woman, walked toward Claire.

"Alex, can you go with Vern, take this guy downtown and get him processed? I'll stay here and go through the house with the owner."

She extended her hand. Claire, still seething and inexplicably relieved that it was the woman staying behind, accepted the handshake.

"I'm Officer Kate Bradshaw."

"I'm Claire DeAngelo. This is my home, and that—" She waved at the car pulling away. "That scumbag is my ex-husband."

"He told us his name is Donald Robinson."

"That's right. Have you…I don't know…arrested him?"

She didn't answer the question. "He told us he doesn't live here. That would make this break-and-enter."

Break-and-enter. The exact words Luke had used that night when Donald came to the condo. The man she had once been married to, thought she had been in love with, had become a stranger. And a criminal.

"I hope you lock him up and throw away the key."

A hint of a smile twitched on Officer Bradshaw's lips. "Is it okay if I go back inside with you so we can go through the place together? He wasn't in there for long, but I'd like you to make sure everything is where it should be, that nothing's missing. And I'll need to get a little more information from you."

"Of course. Come in."

Kate Bradshaw followed her up the steps and waited while she unlocked the front door.

"Nice place," the woman said after she followed Claire inside. "Have you lived here long?"

That was an odd question. "No. Just a few days, actually."

"So it's your place. Mr. Robinson has never lived here with you?"

"No." The second question made the first one sound a little more appropriate. "He has never lived here, and he's not welcome here."

Kate Bradshaw jotted notes. She was maybe five-foot-five, slender but solid-looking, and very, very pretty. Claire wondered if she had pulled her gun on Donald before she'd handcuffed him. It would serve him right. Maybe this time he'd learn his lesson.

"Do you know if Mr. Robinson has ever had any prior criminal charges or convictions?"

"He never mentioned anything like that."

"And where did you live before you moved here?"

Another odd question. Claire gave her the address and watched her write it down.

"How long have you and Mr. Robinson lived apart?"

"Almost a year."

"I see." She flipped her notebook shut. "Let's take a look around. You can let me know me know if you notice anything's missing. And we'll check your windows, make sure they're locked."

"The other officer said that's how he got in—"

"That's right. A bedroom window at the back of the house, the room that's empty."

The baby's room. Claire thought she might throw up. They spent nearly half an hour going through the house, made sure the windows were locked and as far as Claire could see, nothing was missing. But Donald was only after one thing, the Beatrix Potter book, and it was still locked in the safe at her office.

"I can tell you why he broke in. His grandmother gave me an extremely rare edition of an old book. It turns out that it's quite valuable and now that we're divorced, he wants it back." That had to be it. How hard up for money was he? He had tracked her down, broken into her house to look for the book and what...? Was he going to steal it from her? For Donald to do something this stupid, he had to be in serious, *deeply* serious financial trouble.

"I see." Kate Bradshaw flipped open her notebook, made some more notes. "And you can prove the book belongs to you?"

"Yes, I still have the gift card that came with the book. My lawyer has seen it and she's confident that if it ever became a legal issue—" and how ironic that it had "—the card proves that it belongs to me."

"I see. So this book has already been an issue?"

"Yes, and it was settled, or at least I thought it had been."

"And there's nothing else he might have been looking for? Jewelry? Rings?"

Did she mean wedding and engagement rings? Claire had given those back with the rest of his things when she'd sent him packing, but this woman didn't need to know that so Claire simply shook her head.

"I need to get down to the precinct with this information. Here's my card," she said, pulling one from her pocket and handing it to Claire. "Please call me if you think of anything else that might be pertinent, or if you notice anything missing. And I'll keep you up-to-date with any developments concerning Mr. Robinson."

"Thank you, I appreciate that."

"And be sure to keep those doors and windows locked."

"Oh, I will." And first thing in the morning she would arrange to have a security system installed.

Kate hesitated, hand on the doorknob. "I hope you don't mind me asking you one more question."

"Go ahead."

"Do you happen to know Luke Devlin?"

Hmm. The earlier questions that had seemed odd were now a little less...odd. "I do. Why do you ask?"

She shrugged. "No particular reason. Your former address looks familiar. Luke was involved in a situation at that complex a couple of weeks ago. He mentioned that he knew someone who lived there, and I thought your name sounded familiar."

"I take it you know Luke, too?"

"We work together."

I'll bet you do. "Luke and I used to be friends. We went to college together."

She hoped it sounded casual, off the cuff, since anything

she said was sure to get back to him. Then it dawned on her that he would hear about the break-in, as well.

Kate opened the door and stepped out. "Things like this can be unnerving. Maybe you have a friend or family member who can come stay with you for a bit?"

"I do." They were probably at the restaurant already. "Thanks."

"Take care."

She shut the door, locked it and went to get her phone. Sam and Kristi would be getting worried, and the last thing Claire felt like doing right now was getting glammed up for a night out on the town.

Chapter Fourteen

Luke watched Norman dump sugar into a cup of coffee, peel open three little creamers and pour those in and stir. They'd been meeting in this little greasy spoon since Norm, nineteen years sober, had taken Luke under his wing at the first AA meeting he'd ever attended. They'd increased these get-togethers since Luke's close call at the liquor store a couple of weeks ago.

Norm sipped his coffee, sighed appreciatively and leaned back in his chair, giving his ample girth some breathing space. "So…how've you been?"

"Good. More or less."

"How 'bout we start with the less?"

Luke had grown up with a father who was absent much of the time and three sheets to wind all of the time. They had never talked, not really, unless he counted his father's negative and often vulgar criticism. A man who asked straight up how he was feeling, how he was doing and zeroed right in on the problem areas, was an anomaly that had taken some getting used to. His initial instinct was still to gloss over, even cover up what he was really feeling. Norm, God love him, cut through his bullshit like a hot knife through butter.

"I miss her."

"Have you been in touch?"

"Not yet." She ignored his text messages so there'd been no point in calling. Now he realized he shouldn't have left it so long, should have tried to see her in person and get her to hear him out.

"The longer you leave it, the harder it gets." Norm drank some more of his coffee. "Ah, that hits the spot."

Luke gulped his black brew, which, after a week of drinking Claire's coffee, now tasted cheap and bitter. "I shouldn't have left it, but I figured she needed space. She was dealing with her divorce, moving into her new place."

"And now?"

And now he worried it might be too late. "I don't know."

"Does thinking about this make you feel like having a drink?"

Luke stared into his cup. "Yeah." Hell yeah.

"Does being with her make you feel like having a drink?"

Luke looked up, connected with his friend's intense scrutiny. "When I was with her, no. It was the furthest thing from my mind."

"Then I guess you know where you need to be." Norm's deep laugh accompanied that bit of wisdom. "See how easy that was?"

What Norm said made total sense, and sounded a lot easier than it was. Claire's forgiveness would be hard won, if he managed to win it at all. And yes, she was good for him, she always had been. He wouldn't have made it through college without her help. But what did he have to offer her? She was smart, sexy, damn successful in her own right. Any man would be lucky to have her, but she sure as hell didn't need one to look after her.

"You're already overthinking this," Norm said. "Sometimes a man's gotta shut that off and just do what he's gotta do."

"You're a wise man, Norm." Luke drained his cup.

Norm reached for his wallet, but Luke held up a hand, tossed a couple of bills on the table. "My treat. Cheaper than seeing a shrink."

The man's expansive chest heaved with laughter. "You're a good kid, Luke. Don't sell yourself short."

They stood, gave each other a one-armed hug that ended with a pat on the back.

"See you at a meeting soon?" Norm asked.

"You bet." Luke pulled his ringing phone from his jacket pocket. The call was from Kate Bradshaw's cell. "It's work," he said. "I have to take this."

He slid back into the booth, watching Norm leave the coffee shop as he answered. "Hey, Kate. What's up?"

"Remember that guy you asked about a couple weeks ago? Donald Robinson?"

The name alone had the hair up on the back of his neck. "Yeah. What about him?"

"We just booked him for break-and-enter."

"Son of a bitch. What'd he break into?" he asked, although he already knew the answer.

"His ex-wife's place. She's a friend of yours?"

"Claire DeAngelo. Yes, she's a friend." Was a friend. "Is she okay?" If that guy touched her...

"She's fine. She wasn't home at the time, but she pulled up just after we arrested him, probably on her way home from work."

Thank God for that. "How did he get in?"

"Through a bedroom window. One of the neighbors saw him."

"What time?" Luke was on his feet and heading for the door.

"Just before five this afternoon."

In broad daylight? Talk about stupid. Luke's initial assessment of the guy was bang on.

"How's she doing? Did she seem okay?"

"Pretty shaken. I stayed with her for a bit, went through the house, made sure everything was secure. Suggested she might want to call someone to come and stay with her a while."

He got up and left the coffee shop. He knew exactly who she would call. Sam and Kristi. "Did you wait until someone showed up?"

"No. I took her statement and we went through the house to see if anything was missing, then I came back to the precinct. Vern and Alex already had him booked."

"Is he still there?" He crossed the street and climbed into his truck.

"You bet he is."

"How long can you keep him?"

"I'm pretty sure we can stall long enough to keep him overnight."

"Good stuff. I owe you one."

"You already owe me one."

"Okay, I owe you two. Thanks for letting me know about this, Kate. I appreciate it."

"No problem. I had a hunch she was someone special."

She was that, all right. "You'll let me know when Robinson's back on the street?"

"You bet."

He ended the call, shoved the phone into his pocket and revved the engine. Norm was right, he thought as he swerved out of the parking lot. Sometimes a man knew what he had to do, and right now Luke knew he had to go to Claire. He hated to think how rattled she must be, but this might be what it took for him to get his foot in the door. Besides, if he didn't go see her, he'd go down to the precinct to see Donald, and that wouldn't end well for either of them.

IT WAS JUST AFTER DUSK and Claire's lights were on, including the porch light, when Luke pulled up in front of her place. A good sign. He wondered if her friends were here with her, and then he wondered how things might play out for him if they were. Had they already formed a united front against him? Or would Claire be reluctant to call him a "smug son of a bitch" in front of her friends? Time would tell.

He took several minutes to sit and study the house. He'd driven by before so he'd seen it, but he'd mostly been on the lookout for her ex so he hadn't given it a really good look. She'd said buying the condo had been mostly Donald's idea and it hadn't suited her. Too stark, way too pretentious. Some of the furniture had looked like it belonged there, while other pieces, the ones that were hers, had been decidedly out of place. Not here, though. He'd bet she and her things fit this house, snug as a glove.

He got out of the truck, let the door quietly click shut and walked through the gate. He climbed the steps as lightly as he could, not wanting to frighten her if she was alone, and rang the bell before he lost his nerve.

There were voices, which meant she wasn't alone, then footsteps, and the door opened. It was her friend Kristi, dressed to kill in a dark red cocktail dress.

"Um, hi. Is Claire here? I was wondering—"

"Come in." She gave him a light-up-the-room kind of smile, not at all what he expected, and swung the door open. "Claire's right here, in the living room."

He stepped into a small foyer and closed the door. So far, so good.

"Kristi? Who is it?" Claire asked.

He'd even missed the sound of her voice.

"Follow me," she said. "It's Luke."

He entered the living room behind Kristi, vaguely aware that the other friend, Sam, sat curled on the sofa, also wearing some kind of fancy dress, but his real attention was on Claire.

He could tell she'd been sitting in an armchair next to the fire, but she was on her feet by the time he entered the room. She looked ghostly pale, but he supposed that was to be expected.

"What are you doing here?"

"I heard about what happened, wanted to make sure you're okay."

"I'm fine. My friends are here, so you should go."

"Actually," Sam said, getting up from the sofa, "would you look at the time? I need to get home before my son goes to bed."

"Me, too." Kristi already had one arm in her coat. "Jenna will be wanting help with homework, and it's nearly the twins' bedtime, too."

Claire glared daggers at them, clearly not wanting to be left alone with him, while their haste to clear out was an obvious ploy to ensure that's exactly what happened. Interesting. They were her friends, but he recognized allies when he saw them. These two were on his side. Good to know.

"Are you sure you can't stay a little longer?" Claire asked.

Sam winked as she slipped past him on her way to the door. "Sorry. I'll call you in the morning."

"We'll let ourselves out. Lock up behind us?" she asked him.

He followed them out, half expecting one or the other

to give him a hint about what he needed to do next, but they couldn't get out the door fast enough. He locked it and went back to the living room.

Claire was back in the armchair, feet tucked up beside her, arms folded. "You shouldn't have come here."

"I was worried about you. I wanted to make sure you're okay," he repeated.

He wanted to pull her into his arms, touch her, taste her, tell her everything would be all right. Instead he sat on the sofa, uninvited but at least she hadn't told him to get out.

"I'm fine."

"Claire, look—"

"No, you look. I'm sure your girlfriend couldn't wait to call and tell you what happened, but she shouldn't have bothered.

His...who? "What are you talking about? I don't have a girlfriend."

The look she gave him suggested she knew otherwise.

What the hell? Did she think...? "Are you talking about Kate?"

"Yes."

"She's not my girlfriend." And now he was really glad he'd never asked her out. That would just be one more thing to explain.

"Then why was she asking weird questions?"

"What kind of weird questions?"

"About me and you, about Donald, about how you used my condo—"

"She said that?" He found it hard to believe Kate would be that loose-lipped.

"Not exactly."

"Then what did she say?"

Claire shrugged and drew her arms around herself even tighter. He hated that the warm, wonderful woman he'd known had shut herself off from him, and hated even more that it was his fault.

"It's not so much what she said as how she said it."

He leaned forward, forearms on his knees. "Kate and I worked together her first year on the force. She's a good cop, and yes, she's easy on the eyes, but I'd just got sober and I knew I shouldn't…so I didn't. Kate and I are just colleagues. And friends, I hope.

"If her questions sounded a little unusual, it's because I asked her to see what she could dig up on Donald. It was right after that first night, when he came into your place and we were…"

The memory of that night stirred something in him, and it must've had a similar effect on her because she regained a little of her color.

"And she found something?"

He nodded. "Just allegations. No convictions. I couldn't give you specifics, and I wasn't sure how you'd react to my checking up on him. And then you let me stay, and I figured it didn't matter because if he did try something, I'd be there to—"

"Protect me? What about being honest? I hate being lied to, even it's just lying by omission."

"I know. I'm sorry." How many other ways were there to say it?

"I don't care anymore."

He winced at that.

"You hinted that Donald might do something, that's why you wanted to move in, but that was really just one lie to cover up another. You let me think you were interested in me when all you wanted was a place to stake out that other apartment."

He was on his feet, across the room and sitting on the ottoman in front of her chair before she had a chance to react.

"Do you honestly believe that?" He pulled her hands into his. "The time we spent together, that was amazing. But I also had to walk a fine line between keeping you completely out of the picture, for your own protection, and not jeopardizing the investigation."

"So you lied, I get it, but you didn't lie to the people you work with. I heard what that guy said, Luke. That you 'sweet-talked that chick upstairs' into letting you move in." She snatched her hands out of his, crossed her arms and tucked her hands out of sight. "And you laughed. You *laughed* and said I didn't have a clue. I heard you."

He knew exactly what he'd said. In the past several weeks he'd relived the regret more times than he could count.

"Claire, I didn't mean any of it."

"You need to move away from me. Go back and sit over there."

He moved, reluctantly. It hurt, a lot, to know she couldn't stand to be close to him, but he also knew he wouldn't get another chance to change her mind. Hard as it was for him to open up about these things, he had to spill his guts.

"I've done a lot of things I'm not proud of. The drinking, the screwing around. Yes, I had a reputation, and I'd be lying if I said I wasn't proud of it. Some of that was my father's influence, some of it was the booze, but most of it was me being an egotistical jerk. Or a 'smug son of a bitch,' as some have said."

The flicker in her eyes told him she recognized those words as her own.

"Even with Sherri, and I have to tell you, those were some of my darkest days, I never let on to anybody that I had feelings for her."

He still didn't know what those feelings were, but they

weren't the same as the ones he felt for Claire now, or even what he'd felt for her back in college. Those old feelings and these new ones weren't the same, either. Good God, why did this have to be so complicated? Way more complicated sober than drunk. So much for having a clear head.

Claire sat across the room, calm and quiet and still strangely pale, apparently unwilling to throw him a line. So he pressed on.

"I never told Sherri I cared about her. It's never been easy for me to do that, and I always blamed it on the way I was brought up. My father criticized my mother and yelled at me, and for the most part she ignored both of us. I grew up hearing a lot of 'I can't stand you' and 'I hate you,' but none of the other…stuff." Stuff? He still had trouble saying the *L*-word, even in a general way.

"I never once heard anyone in my family say 'I love you' to anybody." There. He'd said it, and it shocked the hell out of him. He had never said it to anyone, and not once, not even when he was a kid, had anyone ever said it to him.

Claire was leaning forward in her chair now, with the makings of tears in her eyes.

"Look, don't get me wrong. I'm not asking for sympathy, it's just the only way I know how to make you understand where I was coming from. I couldn't tell you how I felt about you, so I sure as hell wasn't telling anyone else."

"Are you going to tell me now?" she asked, her voice so quiet he barely heard the question.

"I would, if I knew what it was. I liked you a lot when we studied together. You were smart and funny, you were different from the other girls I knew, in a good way, and to be honest…you kinda scared me."

Her lips had just enough smile to give him hope. "I was a mousy, overweight overachiever. Pretty scary, all right."

He would never understand where those ideas came

from but if she'd let him, he would do everything he could to dispel them. "We need to get you a different mirror. You were never any of those things, not on the outside. I thought you were perfect. Too perfect for me, that's for sure."

He tried to ignore the tear that slid down her cheek. He had to because he wasn't finished yet.

"When I saw you a couple of weeks ago, I couldn't believe you agreed to have dinner with me. And then you invited me up and…wow. You didn't scare me, that's for sure."

She laughed and wiped away the tears. "I've never done anything like that, not on a first date. I've always played it safe, and look where that got me. So that night I assumed you wanted something casual and I told myself I was okay with that, so I threw caution to the wind. But when I overheard your conversation, I realized you weren't the only one lying to me. I was lying to myself."

He wanted to go to her and kiss her senseless, but she still looked so vulnerable. Was it too soon? Should he let her make the next move? She answered the question by crossing the room, kneeling in front of him and putting her hands in his.

"I'm so happy you're here, that you were willing to finally share these things with me. Can we start over, maybe take things a little slower?"

"Of course." He kissed her forehead and pushed the "how slow?" question to the back of his mind. He had another chance and this time he wasn't going to blow it.

"Thank you." She kissed him back, lightly on the mouth, and stood up. "Sit, enjoy the fire, I'll make some coffee. I have…um… There's something else we need to talk about."

He let her go, wondering what else she wanted to say but knowing they both needed a few minutes to process everything that had transpired. And it gave him a chance to look around, take in this new place that she had all but fallen in love with before she'd even seen it.

The living room was a good size but still cosy, with a nice fireplace and a bay window where she planned to put a Christmas tree. The wood floors looked to be original but in good shape. He recognized some of the furniture but most appeared to be new. No sign of that hideous black leather sofa. And there were plenty of feminine touches— a vase full of flowers on the mantel, framed photographs of her friends and her family, books neatly stacked on the coffee table.

He absently picked up the one from the top of the pile, thumbed the pages and realized it was filled with names. He flipped it shut. Baby names, according to the title. The book beneath it had a pregnant woman on the cover, her round, bare belly exposed between a short T-shirt and a pair of exercise pants. He set the first book down, picked up the second, read the inscription on the flyleaf.

For Claire and her baby. Congratulations! Love, Sam & Kristi.

Her *baby?* She didn't look pregnant, unless she wasn't far enough along to look pregnant, which could mean several things and he didn't like any of them.

His chest imploded, squeezing the air out of his lungs.

Was it his? The thought scared the hell out of him.

Someone else's? That idea sickened him.

Either way, he'd just sat here spilling guts while she neglected to tell him she was having a baby. That took "lying by omission" to a whole new level.

He was on his feet in the middle of the room, the book still open in his hands, when she came in with the coffee. One look at her and he had his answer.

She set the cups on the table, hands shaking, the contents sloshing.

"You're having a baby?"

There was no color in her face now, and he didn't care. The anger and betrayal were as real as that night in the E.R. with Sherri, but this time they cut deeper, and the wound was salted with fear. By the time he found out about Sherri's pregnancy, there was no longer a baby. This was different. "Is it mine?"

Her nod was barely perceptible.

He closed the book with a snap. "You trick me into getting you knocked up, then you accuse me of lying?"

"Luke—"

"How the hell did this happen? I asked, remember? And you told me you were on the Pill."

"I was. It wasn't until the next morning that I realized I'd missed quite a few—"

"How many?"

"Almost a week."

"God, Claire. A week? And you kept having sex with me?" Some might call that irresponsible but for him? Irresponsible wasn't even close.

"No. I saw my doctor that day and she recommended using a diaphragm until the end of my cycle. So it was just that one night…"

"Oh, well, I feel so much better. Especially knowing you didn't trust me enough to say something at the time."

"I was afraid to. You had already told me about Sherri and how much you resented what she did, and you made a point of telling me you didn't ever want a family."

His gaze intensified. "So if I hadn't come here tonight, hadn't stumbled on this myself, when were you going to tell me? At least I assume you plan to go through with it since you're already picking out names."

"I...I'm not sure. I just found out a couple of days ago and I knew you'd freak out, but then you came here tonight and we talked and—"

He swung away and stared into the fire, unable to look at her. "And you thought a goddamned cup of coffee would make this easier to swallow?"

She didn't respond, and when he faced her again, she was chalk-white and shaking.

What should he do now? There were no good options that he could see, so the only thing he could do was get the hell out of here before he said or did something he would regret. "I can't do this, not tonight. I'll call you tomorrow."

He didn't slam the door on his way out, but the wreath rattled anyway.

Home sweet home.

Right now that seemed like the biggest lie of all.

Chapter Fifteen

Stunned, Claire flipped the dead bolt shut and leaned against the front door. What was she going to do now?

"I think I'm going to be sick." She covered her mouth with her hand, turned and ran to the bathroom.

Several minutes later, still on her knees, she flushed the toilet and hauled herself to her feet. After she rinsed her mouth and dragged a cool, damp cloth across her face, she looked at herself in the mirror.

"So this is what death warmed over looks like."

And so much for morning sickness living up to its name. She'd felt a little off all day, but this was the first time she had actually thrown up and it was…she checked her watch…almost eight-thirty in the evening. She'd read in the book that morning sickness could happen anytime of day and that some women didn't have it at all, but she had assumed that if she was going to feel this way, it would start in the morning. The past few hours had felt just like a roller coaster, though. Those made her sick, too.

Now Luke knew the truth, had stormed out feeling angry and betrayed, and who could blame him? All because he'd found that stupid book before she'd had a chance to tell him herself. They had just smoothed things out, and now they were worse than ever. And she was sick, and tired, and looked like hell.

She went into the kitchen, put some soda crackers on a plate, poured herself a glass of water and carried them into the living room. Trying to ignore the light-headedness, she snuggled into an afghan and hoped the warmth of the fire would stop the shivering. She picked up a cracker and nibbled on the corner, then washed it down with a sip of water.

Luke said he would call tomorrow. Would he be calmer by then, or even angrier? Either way, they didn't have much more to say to one another. No matter how many times she apologized and tried to explain, he would never forgive or trust her again. And his not wanting a child didn't make her any less pregnant. When he was ready to talk, all she could do was hear him out. She at least owed him that, and then she would assure him she didn't expect anything from him.

Keeping her breathing shallow and even, she swallowed hard against the taste of bile in the back of her throat, bit off another piece of cracker and had another sip of water.

And she really needed to take better care of herself. No more skipping meals, although missing dinner tonight was hardly her fault. She could blame Donald for that, and Luke.

Chloe strolled into the room, looped around the coffee table and paused in front of Claire's chair before leaping onto her lap.

"I'm having a lousy night. Did you know I needed some attention?"

The cat arched her back, turned herself in two full circles, then did one complete revolution in the other direction before tucking her paws beneath herself and doing a side-wrap with her tail.

Claire laughed. "I know, I know. You're the one who's being needy." And that was okay. She didn't need anyone to take of her.

She yawned. She'd always believed everyone who said pregnant women had to eat for two, but who knew she'd also be sleeping for two?

"Come on, girl. Time for bed."

LUKE SAT IN HIS TRUCK for what felt like a long time, but when he pulled out his phone to make a call, it was only half past eight. He called Kate Bradshaw for an update.

"Luke. How's your friend?"

"She's fine." It was a rhetorical question and that was the only right answer. "Just checking on where we're at with Robinson."

"We're keeping him overnight. I was going to call but I figured you might, you know, be kind of busy."

Ha. She didn't know the half of it. "Good to know he's off the street. Call me when he's released tomorrow?"

"Will do," Kate said. "Have a nice night." Clearly she thought he was spending the night with Claire, and it was easier to let her believe that than set her straight.

After he disconnected, he poured himself a cup of coffee from the thermos on the seat next to him. After Kate had called to tell him about Donald's arrest, he had stopped at his place to feed Rex, and while he was there he made the coffee and grabbed a warm jacket. If Donald had been released tonight, Luke would have spent the night here to keep an eye on Claire's place.

That wasn't necessary, and now his head was full of questions with no answers, problems with no solutions and accusations with nothing to refute them. He only knew one way handle situations like this and he didn't dare let himself go there. If he went back to that liquor store tonight, there'd be no way he could walk away.

One day at time just didn't cut it right now.

He wasn't a religious man but there were times when only a prayer would do. This was one of those times.

God, grant me the serenity to accept the things I cannot change, the courage to change the things I can and the wisdom to know the difference.

He rested his forehead on the steering wheel and recited the words again, and then he picked up his phone and called Norman.

CLAIRE SET HER WATER and the plate of soda crackers on the nightstand and crawled into bed with her phone and the pregnancy book, intending to read everything she could about morning sickness. Before that she checked her voice mail. There was only one message, from Officer Bradshaw, letting her know Donald was being "detained" overnight. She liked the picture her imagination created of him in a jail cell. Served him right.

She also had two text messages, one from Sam and the other from Kristi.

Did you and Luke work things out? Is he spending the night? xoxo

That was from Kristi.
Sam's message was a little more graphic.

OMG, that man is hot! Hope he's heating things up for you. S.

She replied to both with the same message.

Things did not go well with Luke. TTY tomorrow. C.

She set the phone on the nightstand, picked up a cracker and opened the book to the table of contents.

Her phone rang.

"What happened?" Sam asked.

"He explained everything about the undercover operation, and I believed him."

"But you wouldn't forgive him?" Kristi asked. Apparently Sam had linked them with a conference call. "Why not?"

"Oh, I did. We talked and agreed to take things a little slower this time. And everything was okay until I went into the kitchen to make coffee and came back to find him looking at the pregnancy books you gave me."

"Oh, no!" Sam said.

"Where were they?" Kristi asked.

"On the coffee table."

"You should have told them they were mine," Sam said.

"There was no point. He'd already read the inscription. I knew he'd be angry, but I never imagined this."

"Sweetie, you had to expect he'd be shocked," Kristi said. "Even angry."

"Of course, but he accused me of deceiving him, and then he accused me of lying to him, and then he stormed out. Oh, and then I threw up."

"Oh, dear. I can relate to that," Sam commiserated. "How are you feeling now?"

"I'm okay. Exhausted, though. I'm already in bed."

"What do you think will happen with Luke?" Kristi asked.

Claire wished she knew. "Honestly, I'm not sure. Before he slammed out of here, he said he couldn't talk to me tonight. He said he'd call me tomorrow, but I'm not sure if there's much point. He doesn't want a family, so there's no possible way this is going to work."

"He said that?" Sam asked. "He definitely doesn't want kids?"

"Several times, and he isn't going to change his mind."

"I wouldn't be so sure," Kristi said. "The guy's crazy about you. You should have seen him when I answered the door tonight. He was so worried. If I hadn't opened it when I did, he might have broken it down."

Claire rolled her eyes at the ceiling. "Just what I need. Two break-ins in one day."

Sam laughed.

"Okay, you know I was exaggerating. What I'm saying is that I've seen guys in love, and this guy has it bad."

"Kristi's right. Give him time, give him space if he needs it, but don't slam the door just yet."

Luke had already slammed it, literally and figuratively. "I'll see what he has to say tomorrow, but I'm not counting on him having a change of heart.

"What about Donald?" Kristi asked. "Would you like us to come back and spend the night?"

"Just say the word," Sam added.

"He won't be released until tomorrow." She still had trouble wrapping her head around that.

"That's a relief," Kristi said.

Sam simply let out a whoop.

"I'll be fine here on my own. I love you guys."

"Will you call us tomorrow after you've talked to Luke?"

"I will, I promise."

LUKE SPENT THE FIRST half of the night with a pot of coffee and the TV remote, and the second half lying in bed in the dark waiting to nod off. Sleep eluded him, and by dawn he knew this would be a lousy day. Maybe the lousiest on record.

That was confirmed when he threw on a load of laundry, a hose or a seal or something went on the washing machine, and water leaked all over the utility room floor. He was mopping up the mess when Kate called to let him know Stalker Don was out on bail. And then Norm called, insisting they meet for coffee.

Luke didn't want to see anyone, he really didn't want any more coffee and he sure as hell didn't need a lecture on the dangers of having a drink or having sex without a condom.

Norm wasn't taking no for answer and, as he always did, he managed to say exactly what Luke needed to hear. Luke had started out not wanting to hear any of those things, but Norm didn't give a rat's ass about that. And that, Luke thought wryly, was an exact quote.

He'd taken Norm's advice and called Claire, just as he'd said he would. She answered, and he didn't know whether to be surprised by that or not. He suggested they get together for coffee…what the hell, it wasn't like he was ever going to sleep again…and she had agreed.

He knew better than to suggest her place, this would be better done in public, someplace where they, well, mostly he would be on his best behavior. No chance of theatrics like the raised voice and door slamming he'd been guilty of last night. Claire had agreed to meet him and suggested a place near her office in Pioneer Square.

He arrived half an hour early and was nursing his second cup of coffee when, through the window, he caught a glimpse of her crossing the street. She would always be the one woman who would turn his head, not only because she was beautiful, but also because she had always been able to cut through his crap. Maybe if he'd paid more attention, he'd have figured out how to cut through hers.

CLAIRE HAD TRIED ON half a dozen outfits before she left for the office that morning, but as she went to meet Luke, she was having serious second thoughts. Instead of one of the suits she usually wore, she'd decided on dark jeans and a black turtleneck sweater under the cobalt-blue jacket she'd worn the first time they'd gone out. Marlie had been surprised to see her dressed so casually, but she had assured her that she didn't have any appointments that day. Technically true, since she had already rescheduled them.

Now, as she crossed the street to the coffee shop where she, Sam and Kristi met for their weekly business meetings, she had second thoughts. She wanted to show Luke that she could be as cool and casual as he was, but she was more herself in a suit. More polished and professional, and a lot more confident. She should have gone with that.

Too late now, she thought as she opened the door and went in to face the music. She spotted him right away, and her heart did that skip-a-beat thing it always did. He was wearing his leather jacket, his helmet on the seat next to him. Now she really wished she'd worn a suit. Not that it would make her heart behave, but it might disguise its misbehavior.

He saw her, too, and his detached gaze suggested that although he could see her, he would rather not look at her.

She stopped at the counter and ordered a decaf latte, then reluctantly crossed the narrow space and joined Luke at the back corner table he'd chosen. He leaned back in his chair, watching her like she was a petty criminal. He had a lot of nerve.

She set her briefcase on the floor next to her chair, still not sure why she'd bothered to bring it but willing to acknowledge it was part of that professional facade she wished she'd gone with. Right now the only thing that gave her the upper hand was waiting for him to be the first to speak.

"How are you?"

"I'm fine."

"Did you hear Donald's out?"

"I got a call this morning." She should have known that Kate Bradshaw would call Luke, too.

"You should think about getting a security alarm."

One step ahead of you. "I have a company coming this afternoon to give me an estimate."

"That's good."

The barista set her latte on the table in front of her, table service being one of the perks of being a regular customer.

"Thank you," she said, not missing the young woman's appreciative assessment of Luke.

If he noticed, he didn't let on.

She sipped her drink and a few seconds of silence ticked into ten, twenty…

"I'm sorry about the way I behaved last night," he said, running a hand through his hair. He looked tired, she noticed, as though he hadn't slept well.

"I'm sorry you had to find out the way you did. Not that there was a good way to tell you."

"What happens now?" His question was so direct, it caught her by surprise.

"Nothing has to happen. I know how you feel about kids."

"So you're planning to go through with this?"

Go through with *this?* He couldn't even bring himself to say the words. *Pregnancy. Baby.*

She could be as direct as he was. "I am."

He leaned forward, forearms on the table, coffee cup cradled in both hands. "Last night, after two weeks of ignoring my messages, you let me back in your life. You said you wanted to take things slow. Since you knew you were pregnant and I didn't want kids, exactly how did you think that was going to work?"

How this worked was really up to him. "I'm not sure, Luke. Last night I was going to tell you myself, and I was prepared for you to be upset—"

"Upset? Jeez, Claire…" He seemed to catch himself, lowered his voice. "I get 'upset' when I get a flat tire or the damn washing machine breaks down. Getting a woman pregnant the first time I sleep with her, that freaks me out."

"You didn't 'get me' pregnant. That was my fault."

"It's mine, that makes me responsible."

It *is a baby,* she wanted to remind him.

"You should have said something as soon as you knew. I mean, there were options."

Now she was angry. "I'm very well aware of the options. I've already chosen one."

His expression finally registered the reality of the situation. "You really plan to go through with this?"

"I told you I do." She couldn't tell him this might be her only chance to have a baby. That had nothing to do with him, and he would never understand anyway. "That's my decision, which makes it my responsibility."

He looked bewildered. "Do you want to get married?"

"Is that a proposal?"

He shoved his cup away. "It's a question."

A dumb question, she thought. "And the answer is no. I don't."

He slowly reached into his pocket, pulled out a folded piece of paper and slid it across the table to her. "This is the best I can do right now."

She didn't have to unfold it to know it was a check, but she had to ask. "What's this for?"

He shrugged. "Whatever you and…whatever the two of you need."

He was offering money? This was his solution? Curiosity being what it was, she picked it up, opened it and was pretty sure she gasped. It was payable to her, in the amount of ten thousand dollars.

So this was it? Throw money at the problem and make it go away?

She refolded it, set it on the table and made a show of slowly sliding it back.

He watched with narrowed eyes. "What are you doing?"

"I'm not trying to land a husband, and I'm not looking for money."

"What do you want?"

"Nothing." Just as well, since he couldn't give it to her anyway.

"There has to be something."

Since she had nothing to lose, she told him. "I'll tell you what I want. It's all or nothing, Luke. With kids, there's no halfway. You're either in or you're out."

"But—"

She cut him off. "I have a home, money, a stable career. I'm perfectly capable of raising a child on my own and providing everything she or he needs."

The only thing worse than no father was a reluctant one. This was his loss, even though she couldn't bring herself to say it. She didn't want to hurt him, she just wanted him to go away and let her get on with her life. And she needed to take the first step.

She reached for her briefcase and stood up, actually grateful that Luke was at a loss for words.

"If you ever change your mind, you know where to find me." And she walked away from the one thing she wanted even more than a baby—the man who'd given her one.

Chapter Sixteen

Luke spent the next four days alternating between anger, disappointment and relief. The only constants were the struggle to stay sober and the feeling that he was a bigger jerk now than he'd ever been. After Claire told him it was "all or nothing"—and since she didn't want financial support or marriage, he didn't have a clue what that meant—he had talked with Jason Wong and taken a leave of absence. One thing was certain. In his current state of mind, he was no good to anybody.

This morning, like every morning since Claire's ultimatum, he joined Norman at the coffee shop.

"How's it going?" Norm asked.

"Good."

"I didn't ask how you are, I asked how it's going."

Luke knew what the question was. "Somewhere on the road between step four and step ten, with a stopover at eight." Except the moral inventory wasn't so fearless, and while he figured he was more than willing to make amends, he still hadn't figured out what he'd done wrong.

"It is a journey, all right."

Luke rolled his eyes. "That's the best you've got?"

Norm laughed. "How are you sleeping these days?"

"Better."

"That's good. What are you doing to keep yourself busy now that you're not working?"

He shrugged, feeling a little a kid who'd forgotten to take out the trash. "Watching TV, taking Rex for a run. I fixed the washing machine."

"Driven past Claire's place?"

It was the first time Norm had mentioned her since Luke told him about the baby. Why would he ask if Luke was keeping an eye on her? And how the hell did he know he was? Norm was smiling, like he knew everything.

"A time or two." Every day. To make sure Donald wasn't hanging around.

"Do you love her?" Norm asked.

"I don't know. I'm pretty sure I've never been in love so it's hard to tell."

"Let's forget about the baby for a minute. Do you think about her very often?"

"All the time."

"Is that right? So when you're doing all this thinking, is it all about the sex?"

"Jeez, Norm. What kind of question is that?"

"Just answer it, and be honest."

Honestly, he did think about the sex, it was amazing, but more often she occupied his thoughts in other ways. "It's more about the things she's said, or how she takes her glasses off and cleans them on her sleeve, or watching her in the kitchen. She's a really good cook, did I mention that? Best lasagna I've ever had."

"Huh." Norm had sat quiet for a few moments, drinking his coffee and no doubt pondering his next question. "You think about her all the time and it's hardly ever about the sex. But you've had a lot of women, right?"

Luke had glanced around the coffee shop, hoping no one overheard.

"Just answer the question," Norm said.

"I've had my share."

"And you've felt this way about how many of them? All of them? Some of them? Say, half of them, maybe."

Luke didn't know where Norm was going with this, but there was only one honest answer.

"None of them."

"Huh. So she occupies every waking thought. Maybe even a dream or two, I'll bet, since you're sleeping okay. It's not just about the sex, and she's different from any other woman you've ever met. One of a kind." Norm paused to polish off his coffee. "Did you see that light-bulb come on?" he asked.

"Yeah, I did." Bright as a beacon.

"That, my friend, is love. Now the only question is, what are you going to do about it? Let it go because you're afraid you can't live up to your responsibilities? Or take a shot at being the luckiest man alive?"

"I always liked the sound of lucky."

"Then do it. You're going to make a great dad."

Luke still wasn't sure about that. He was just getting used to the idea of being in love. "Why didn't you ask me all these questions a couple of days ago?"

"Figured you weren't ready to answer them."

"What's different today?"

"Figured you were ready."

Damn. Norm was right, he was ready. He didn't know how long it would have taken to reach that conclusion on his own but now that he had, he needed to find a way to convince Claire.

"Any suggestions where to go from here?"

Norm pulled out his wallet and paid for their coffees. "Sorry, kid. You're on your own."

"I was afraid you were going to say that." But even as he said it, the plan started to form. Now he needed to make it work.

IT TOOK HIM NEARLY A week to work out the details, but the plan had finally come together. He didn't know if it was a good plan or if it was even going to work, but it was the only thing he could come up with. Now it was time to put it to the test.

"Come on, Rex. We're going for a ride."

He put the dog in the front seat with him, tossed the package on the dashboard and set off for Claire's. He hadn't seen her since the morning they'd met for coffee, but he'd finally figured out what she meant by in or out, all or nothing.

Although he was still on leave, he'd been relieved to hear from Kate Bradshaw that Claire's problems with Donald had been resolved. In exchange for not being charged for breaking into her home, he had signed an affidavit forfeiting any claim to Claire's book. There was also a restraining order in effect, but because the condo was sold and the book was no longer an issue, they didn't expect any more trouble. When questioned about his motive for wanting to steal the book, it had come out that he and his new girlfriend had been living the high life, and he was deep in debt to a couple of loan sharks. That was his problem, not Claire's.

Luke knew she'd be home because he had talked to her friends, Sam and Kristi, and they had helped him set this up. Claire thought they were dropping by to help with some decorating project. Instead she was getting him.

She was on the veranda sanding an old piece of furniture, and she didn't notice him pull up. Chloe sat in the bay window inside, not missing a trick.

"Rex, stay," he said as he got out. He grabbed the package off the dashboard, though, and tucked it under his arm.

She looked up from her work and saw him when he got to the gate.

He had hoped to see her smile, but she only looked surprised.

"I really must have been concentrating on what I was doing. I didn't hear your motorcycle pull up."

"I'm not on the bike."

"You have your truck?" She scanned the street for it.

"No. I sold it."

"Is that—?" She pointed to the shiny new SUV with Rex sitting in the front seat. "Is that yours?"

"It is." He opened the gate and walked toward her.

"You bought an SUV?" She set the sanding block on the top of an old dresser and came down the steps to meet him.

"Traded the truck and the Ducati for it."

"You sold your bike? Luke, you love that bike."

"As it turns out, there's something I love more."

"Is there? And what would that be?"

"You."

Her mouth softened into a smile and it was all he could do to resist kissing her.

"What made you change your mind?" she asked.

"You have to remember I'm not as smart as you are, so it took me a while to figure out what it means to be all-in."

"And now you know?"

"I do. Actually, I think I was close before. I really would have married you, supported you, if you'd let me. But I was missing a step."

"Which step was that?"

"Saying I love you."

"Is that what you're saying now?" Trust Claire to not make this easy.

"I'm saying I love you, Claire DeAngelo." There. He said it, and he meant it, and he would never forget the way she was looking at him right now.

She took his hand and laced her fingers with his. "I love you, too, Luke Devlin. I think I always have."

Yep, Norm was right. He was the luckiest man alive.

"There's more," he said.

"More than loving me and wanting to… I'm sorry, why exactly did you buy an SUV?"

"Because I'm all-in, Claire. I want to marry you and have a baby with you, and this has the highest safety rating of any vehicle on the market right now."

She laughed. "Usually when a guy asks a girl to marry him, he buys her a ring, not the safest SUV on the market."

"Oh, I'm not *asking* you to marry me right now. I just said I *want* to marry you. Besides, I thought we were taking things slow."

"Fair enough."

"I have something else for you, though."

"A pre-engagement present?"

"Sure." He gave her the package and watched her while she examined it.

"It's a book."

"I know what it is. Are you going to open it?"

"Of course I am. I'm just savoring the moment." She carefully unstuck the tape and removed the wrapping without a single rip.

"The Tale of Benjamin Bunny." The way she ran her hand over the cover was practically reverent. "And it's a first edition. Luke, where did you find it?"

"Online. I had it shipped by courier." He'd been worried it wouldn't arrive for him to give it to her today, but his luck had held. "When I helped you pack your books, you said you'd like to have a first edition someday."

"I can't believe you remembered. Thank you." She put her arms around his neck and kissed him, and he went from being the luckiest man alive to the happiest. "I love the book. And I love you."

He held her close, this incredible woman who had his child growing inside her, this amazing woman who knew all of his flaws and loved him anyway. He wanted this to last forever.

"Let's get Rex and go inside," she said.

Rex leapt out of the SUV and dashed through the gate, excited to see Claire, but when he caught sight of Chloe standing in the window, arched and hissing, the poor guy dropped to the ground and covered his nose.

Claire knelt, blocking his view of the window. "Come on inside, Rex. Would you like a treat?"

He bounded up the stairs to the front door.

"I'm glad you brought him. Rex and Chloe need to work out their differences," she said, standing and taking his hand again.

"Like we did?"

"Yes, like we did." She gazed up at the house, then back at him. "Now that the two of you are here, this house will finally feel like home."

Home sweet home. The phrase finally made sense to him. They climbed the front steps and went inside together. Someday he would carry her across this threshold, but for today this was enough.

Epilogue

Six months later...

Claire carried the cake, decorated with soft pink rosebuds and ribbons of pale green icing, into the dining room and set it in the center of the table. Luke had put in all the leaves to extend the table to accommodate everyone, and they would all be here soon.

"Now will you please sit down?" he asked. "Even if it's just for five minutes."

"If I sit down, I may never get up again." She had two months to go before the babies would be here, and her body had all the grace and proportions of a beached whale. But every day Luke told her that she was the most beautiful mother-to-be on the planet, and she was more than happy to have him as her mirror.

He guided her into her favorite armchair in the living room. "Don't move. I'll be right back with a decaf latte."

And so she sat with nothing to do but admire the vases of pink roses and baby's breath she'd scattered around the room. Today's baby shower was for Sam and AJ and their new baby daughter, Rose. Kristi and Nate and their family were coming, too.

Claire gently rubbed her bulging belly, feeling a foot here, an elbow there. Four months ago she and Luke had found out they were having twins, and while the surprise had worn off, the shock hadn't. Kristi, who was raising twin stepdaughters, said it would probably last until they left for college.

Luke, her devoted husband, set her cup on the side table. "Thank you. I keep thinking how nice it will be to have real coffee again."

"It won't be long now." He sat on the arm of her chair and his hand joined hers in an exploration of her belly and the protruding baby appendages.

Car doors slammed outside, followed by the sound of voices and footsteps on the veranda. Claire got to her feet, excited to greet their friends, who were really their extended family at the door.

"So much for you having a rest."

She kissed his cheek, then ran her hand over the light stubble on his jaw. "The doctor says I'm healthy and the babies are healthy. We're all fine, and I can rest later."

She had wanted to throw this party for Sam, to celebrate the arrival of her new baby, but mostly she wanted to do it for herself. She had her dream home, complete with white picket fence, and the person who'd been the man of her dreams all her adult life shared it with her. And they would soon have the family she had always longed for. With so much love in one house, it would be a shame not to share it. She wasn't sure if Luke agreed with her or just humored her, but either way she loved him for it.

Luke helped her to her feet and together they greeted their friends.

Kristi and Nate trooped in with their five-year-old twin daughters, Molly and Martha, bouncing ahead of them and their teenage daughter, Jenna, straggling behind and tapping out a text message on her iPhone.

"Claire's living room is a gadget-free zone," Kristi reminded her.

Jenna rolled her eyes, stuck her phone in her pocket and hugged Claire.

"It's Luke's rule," Claire whispered to her, eliciting a laugh.

Behind them, Sam and AJ appeared in the doorway, with their four-year-old son, Will, between them and the baby carrier in AJ's hand.

"Oh, Sam. She's beautiful."

Sam gave her a warm hug. "See what you have to look forward to?"

"Times two," Kristi said.

"I can't wait."

Everyone shed coats and jackets, and while the children dashed out to the backyard and Jenna retreated to the dining room with her phone, the grown-ups settled into the living room.

Sam answered questions about how well the baby was sleeping and AJ told them about the last checkup with the pediatrician and how much weight she'd gained.

Then it was Claire's turn to share the news of her last prenatal exam and Luke told everyone he thought the doctor should have told her to take things easy.

That made everyone laugh, and then Kristi took Nate's hand. "While we're on the subject of babies…"

"Omigosh! You're pregnant, too?" Sam hugged her. "Congratulations!"

"More babies!" Claire said, clapping her hands together. "I'd hug you, too, but I can't get up."

"A baby," Nate said, grinning widely and accepting hearty handshakes from the other dads. "One set of twins is plenty."

One set of twins is perfect, Claire thought.

"If the three of us plan to keep this up," Sam said, "we'll have to come up with a schedule so we're not all on maternity leave at the same time."

Claire joined in the laughter as she gazed around the room at her friends, then up at her husband who sat next to her, one arm around her shoulder. She had to be the luckiest woman alive.

"Ready Set Sold is in the business of creating homes for families," she told them. "I'd say we're managing just fine."

"Home sweet homes," Luke said, seeking out her hand and giving it a squeeze. "That could be your company slogan."

She laced her fingers with his. "It's perfect," she said. Everything was perfect.

* * * * *

COMING NEXT MONTH
from Harlequin® American Romance®

AVAILABLE JUNE 4, 2013

#1453 A COWBOY'S PRIDE
Pamela Britton

An accident changes Trent's world, and Alana is determined to help him. But once he's back on his feet, will he go back to his glamorous rodeo life and leave her behind?

#1454 HIS BABY DREAM
Safe Harbor Medical
Jacqueline Diamond

Widower Peter Gladstone wants a child. He never expected his egg donor, who is supposed to remain anonymous, to become a friend...and more. How can he tell her they may have a baby on the way?

#1455 DESIGNS ON THE COWBOY
Roxann Delaney

Dylan Walker's sister has hired Glory Andrews to renovate his ranch house, and Dylan is not happy about it. The cowboy just wants to be left alone, but Glory is hard to ignore!

#1456 THE RANCHER SHE LOVED
Saddlers Prairie
Ann Roth

When former rodeo champion Clay Hollyer meets up with Sarah Tigarden, the writer who panned him in print, sparks fly—and not the good kind. At first...

You can find more information on upcoming Harlequin® titles, free excerpts and more at www.Harlequin.com.

HARCNM0513

REQUEST YOUR FREE BOOKS!
2 FREE NOVELS PLUS 2 FREE GIFTS!

HARLEQUIN

American ★ Romance®

LOVE, HOME & HAPPINESS

YES! Please send me 2 FREE Harlequin® American Romance® novels and my 2 FREE gifts (gifts are worth about $10). After receiving them, if I don't wish to receive any more books, I can return the shipping statement marked "cancel." If I don't cancel, I will receive 4 brand-new novels every month and be billed just $4.74 per book in the U.S. or $5.24 per book in Canada. That's a savings of at least 14% off the cover price! It's quite a bargain! Shipping and handling is just 50¢ per book in the U.S. and 75¢ per book in Canada.* I understand that accepting the 2 free books and gifts places me under no obligation to buy anything. I can always return a shipment and cancel at any time. Even if I never buy another book, the two free books and gifts are mine to keep forever.

154/354 HDN F4YN

Name _____ (PLEASE PRINT) _____

Address _____ Apt. # _____

City _____ State/Prov. _____ Zip/Postal Code _____

Signature (if under 18, a parent or guardian must sign) _____

Mail to the **Harlequin® Reader Service:**
IN U.S.A.: P.O. Box 1867, Buffalo, NY 14240-1867
IN CANADA: P.O. Box 609, Fort Erie, Ontario L2A 5X3

Want to try two free books from another line?
Call 1-800-873-8635 or visit www.ReaderService.com.

* Terms and prices subject to change without notice. Prices do not include applicable taxes. Sales tax applicable in N.Y. Canadian residents will be charged applicable taxes. Offer not valid in Quebec. This offer is limited to one order per household. Not valid for current subscribers to Harlequin American Romance books. All orders subject to credit approval. Credit or debit balances in a customer's account(s) may be offset by any other outstanding balance owed by or to the customer. Please allow 4 to 6 weeks for delivery. Offer available while quantities last.

Your Privacy—The Harlequin® Reader Service is committed to protecting your privacy. Our Privacy Policy is available online at www.ReaderService.com or upon request from the Harlequin Reader Service.

We make a portion of our mailing list available to reputable third parties that offer products we believe may interest you. If you prefer that we not exchange your name with third parties, or if you wish to clarify or modify your communication preferences, please visit us at www.ReaderService.com/consumerchoice or write to us at Harlequin Reader Service Preference Service, P.O. Box 9062, Buffalo, NY 14269. Include your complete name and address.

HAR13R

SPECIAL EXCERPT FROM

HARLEQUIN®

American ★ Romance®

A COWBOY'S PRIDE

by Pamela Britton

A wounded cowboy. His gorgeous physical
therapist. What could go wrong?

"Welcome to the New Horizons Ranch," Rana Jensen said,
tipping up on her toes in excitement.

No response.

Alana McClintock recognized Trent Anderson from watching
him on TV. It looked as if he hadn't shaved in a few days, his
jaw and chin covered by at least a week's worth of stubble.

"Good to see you, Trent," Cabe called out.

No response.

Tom hopped inside the bus and released the wheelchair. And
suddenly the longtime rodeo hero was face-to-face with the
small crowd who'd gathered to greet him.

"Welcome to New Horizons Ranch," Rana repeated happily.

Still no response.

The cowboy didn't so much as lift his head.

Tom pushed the wheelchair onto the lift. Sunlight illuminated
Trent Anderson's form. Still the same broad shoulders and
handsome face. It was his legs that looked different.

"Don't expect much of a conversation from him," said Tom.

"He hasn't spoke two words since I fetched him from the airport. Starting to think he lost his voice along with the use of his legs."

That got a reaction.

"I can still walk," Trent muttered.

Barely from what she'd heard. Partial paralysis of both legs from midthigh down. There'd been talk he'd never walk again. The fact that he had some feeling in his upper legs was a miracle.

"I'll show you to your cabin, Mr. Anderson," Rana said, coming forward.

"Don't touch me." He spun the aluminum frame around. "I can do it myself."

Alana took one look at Rana's crushed face and jumped in front of the man.

"*You* have no idea where you're going." She placed her hands on her hips and dared him to try and run her down.

"I'll find my way."

He swerved around her.

She met Cabe's gaze, then looked over at the bus driver. They both stared at her with a mix of surprise and dismay. "First cabin on the left." She stepped to the side. "Don't let the front door hit you in the butt."

Three stunned faces gazed back at her, though she didn't bother looking at Trent again. Yeah, she might have sounded harsh, but the man was a jerk.

Too bad she would have to put up with him for three weeks.

Be sure to look for A COWBOY'S PRIDE from Harlequin American Romance. Available June 4, 2013, wherever Harlequin books are sold!

Copyright © 2013 by Pamela Britton

HAREXP0613

HARLEQUIN®

American ★ Romance®

Peter Gladstone may have lost his beloved wife, but the
tragedy has only strengthened his resolve to create a
family. With a donor egg and a surrogate mom in place,
Peter is sure to be a proud papa soon. The only problem
is, Peter sees his egg donor Harper Anthony as a friend…
and maybe something more. And Peter has chosen to
keep his donor identity a secret. If the truth comes out,
the consequences may threaten their budding romance.
But only the truth can turn them into a family…

His Baby Dream

by JACQUELINE DIAMOND

**Available June 4 from
Harlequin® American Romance®.**

www.Harlequin.com

HAR75458